"I take it my brother sent you?" Marit asked.

"He would like you to return to Svardia."

Instinctively she took a step back. "I have every intention of doing so, but first—"

"*Un*wed," the man all but growled, taking a single step toward her, returning the distance to what it had been.

Fire scorched her. *No.* She couldn't return to Svardia until she was married. If not, then Aleksander would have to choose a husband for her. A stranger for her. And she couldn't let that happen.

"No."

"Yes."

"I can imagine it easily escaped the notice of one of my brother's minions—"

"*Minion,*" the man repeated as if it were some great insult.

"—but this is the twenty-first century and—"

Her words cut short the moment he swept into the room, stalking toward her in such a way that had her stepping back again, or at least trying to. Her heel tangled in the hundredth layer of tulle, and swaying dangerously on the other foot, she was about to go down, when the man appeared before her, bent down and, to Princess Marit of Svardia's utter shock, hoisted her over his shoulder.

Pippa Roscoe

STOLEN FROM HER ROYAL WEDDING

HARLEQUIN®
PRESENTS™

Recycling programs
for this product may
not exist in your area.

ISBN-13: 978-1-335-56869-4

Stolen from Her Royal Wedding

Copyright © 2022 by Pippa Roscoe

All rights reserved. No part of this book may be used or reproduced in
any manner whatsoever without written permission except in the case of
brief quotations embodied in critical articles and reviews.

This is a work of fiction. Names, characters, places and incidents
are either the product of the author's imagination or are used fictitiously.
Any resemblance to actual persons, living or dead, businesses,
companies, events or locales is entirely coincidental.

For questions and comments about the quality of this book,
please contact us at CustomerService@Harlequin.com.

Harlequin Enterprises ULC
22 Adelaide St. West, 41st Floor
Toronto, Ontario M5H 4E3, Canada
www.Harlequin.com

Printed in U.S.A.

Pippa Roscoe lives in Norfolk near her family and makes daily promises to herself that this is the day she'll leave the computer to take a long walk in the countryside. She can't remember a time when she wasn't dreaming about handsome heroes and innocent heroines. Totally her mother's fault, of course—she gave Pippa her first romance to read at the age of seven! She is inconceivably happy that she gets to share those daydreams with you all. Follow her on Twitter, @pipparoscoe.

Books by Pippa Roscoe

Harlequin Presents

Rumors Behind the Greek's Wedding
Playing the Billionaire's Game

Once Upon a Temptation

Taming the Big Bad Billionaire

The Diamond Inheritance

Terms of Their Costa Rican Temptation
From One Night to Desert Queen
The Greek Secret She Carries

The Royals of Svardia

Snowbound with His Forbidden Princess

Visit the Author Profile page
at Harlequin.com for more titles.

This one is for Tony and Chris,

Dale and Bertie, Bob and Greg.

And for Brenda, Kylie and Gale.

It was worth it, I promise, and I can't thank you enough.

xx

CHAPTER ONE

MARIT PRESSED A hand against the white corset of the wedding dress in an attempt to calm the unease sweeping across her stomach. Her heart fluttered in her chest, not with the nerves of an eager bride but with the fear that she was about to make a terrible mistake. Until she remembered exactly why she was doing this. The hand at her stomach formed into a fist. She had made her decision. It might be the last reckless act of the youngest Svardian Princess, but it was important. She knew what she was doing.

Liar.

The voice sounded very much like Freya's. Marit's heart thudded guiltily in her chest at the thought of the older sister who had been more like a mother to her than their own. No, Princess Freya most definitely would *not* approve of what Marit was about to do.

She looked at her reflection in the hotel room's mirror and clenched her jaw when she saw her lip trembling. Shouldn't a mother be present on her daughter's wedding day? Shouldn't family be gathered? Friends?

Inhaling slow and deep, Marit turned a critical eye on the off-the-shelf wedding dress she and André had bought in the Parisian boutique yesterday afternoon. The sweetheart neckline gaped a little and the dress looked too big for her. The skirt, made of layers and layers and layers of tulle, swamped her and there was something about the colour…the startling white made her look pallid.

It's not the dress, Marit.

When Aleksander, her older brother and King of Svardia, had called her to his office in Rilderdal Palace two weeks ago, she thought he'd found out about her secret project. That perhaps one of his palace spies had told him about her plans to create an inner city youth orchestra. Marit might not have been allowed to study music at university, but she could never have walked away from it. She'd kept the venture a secret because her family—her *parents*—would have expected her to fail. Just like they had ever since she'd been an awkward young princess tripping over her own feet, or spilling chocolate sauce on her gown just minutes before the yearly Christmas family photograph, or later, nearly causing an international incident because she had forgotten the correct etiquette with the Taiwanese delegation.

So, two weeks ago, Marit had sat in the King of Svardia's office—a jarring clash of the latest technology and original baroque interior design—mentally mounting a defence of the youth project she'd been working on for eight months since leaving university.

And when her brother had said, 'Freya will be stepping down. She has no choice. And neither do you. You will now be second in line to the throne,' she'd not heard him at first. But her heart had.

It understood, far more quickly than her brain, the precarious position she was now in and, caught between fight or flight, the organ had stopped. Her body's need for survival had been the only thing that forced a powerful, loud, crashing thud of a beat through her heart to restart it. Her brother's dominant gaze had needled into her awareness, forcing understanding through her shocked mind. There had been no choice. No discussion. It simply was.

She had met her sister outside her brother's office, tears gathering in Freya's beautiful amber eyes, and they had crashed together in an embrace that conveyed the depth and desperation of their love and their fears. Freya was the most loving and generous person Marit had ever known and that she would never be able to carry a child to term was devastating. But that Freya felt she could not remain second in line to the throne because she was not able to produce the spare heirs required to protect the future of the Svardian monarchy felt unbearably cruel. Freya loved what she did with a passion Marit could only ever compare to her own love of music. And Marit feared the loss of that role on top of the children Freya had wanted so much might just be too much for her sister to bear.

Marit's grief for Freya's loss was a seething dark, aching thing. But her greatest shame was the twist of selfishness within it that ached for her own loss: *her* freedom. Through the years it had been made painfully clear that Marit was surplus to requirements. She might have received the required royal training but no one had ever expected, or wanted, her to be involved in royal duties. And the role that Freya was leaving was frankly intimidating to the Princess who had been proclaimed The Rebellious Royal by every single international broadsheet. There had never been any question of her refusing her King's command. Marit would *never* abandon her brother or sister in such a way. But there was one last act of rebellion she had left to do. As second in line to the throne, she would have to marry a man with a title, a man of her brother's choosing.

But she just couldn't.

The thought of marrying a stranger, of being intimate with a man she'd never met… Her heart quivered in her chest as her breath stuttered around what she was about to do. Because she wasn't second in line to the throne *yet*. And if she was already married by the time she took her sister's place, then the legislation that had tied the hands of Svardian princesses for generations wouldn't apply to her.

Which was why Marit was standing in front of a mirror in the best suite in *Le Jardin Exquis* in an off-the-shelf wedding dress, about to marry André Du Sault. Her best friend from university, and the only reason she'd scraped a pass on the business de-

gree her parents had insisted she took, understood
why she was doing this. He had his own reasons and
the rest, they'd decided in the short time they'd had
to pull this entire thing together, they would figure
out as they went. But now? Now it was time to get
married.

The sound of a commotion outside the suite drew
her attention to the door, ruffling the layers of the
tulle skirt.

'*Monsieur, arrêtez!* Wait, *monsieur*! You cannot
go in there. *Monsieur!*'

The panicked cries of the hotel's staff were all the
warning Marit had before the door was flung open to
reveal a figure in the doorway with silvery eyes and
a determined jaw, staring at her as if he knew her.

Contrary to popular belief, Lykos Livas was not in
the habit of kidnapping women on their wedding
days. Not that he hadn't, on occasion, enjoyed the
company of a runaway bride or two. But track-
ing down and retrieving a runaway princess in the
heart of Paris on the morning of what she intended
to be her wedding day at the behest of said Princess's brother was hardly a normal start to the day
for Lykos. He checked the address in the message on
his phone and returned the mobile to his ear, leaning back against his silver Aston Martin Vantage.

'Are you sure she's here?' he demanded.

'I'm sure that her *phone* is there, Lykos. As I'm
currently in Norfolk patching drywall—'

'You're what?' Lykos frowned in confusion, unable to imagine Theron Thiakos, CEO of an internationally renowned security company, doing DIY of all things.

'Finally fixing the hole that Summer put in the wall.'

'*Adelfe*, if you and Summer are in the middle of—'

'*Ela*, Lykos, that's the mother of my child,' Theron groused.

'And she's perfect for you,' Lykos soothed in the most patronising tone he could manage.

'*Nai*, she is,' Theron replied smugly, ignoring Lykos's tease. Lykos was happy for the man he had all but grown up with on the streets of Greece. Straining at the constraints of the orphanage in Piraeus, the two had raised merry hell throughout Athens until they had been discovered by Kyros Agyros. That his success was even partly down to the man who had both mentored Lykos and betrayed his trust still stung. But it had been an important lesson to learn and one he'd never forget; the only person in this life that he could trust was himself.

'So, are you going to tell me why you needed me to track the phone of the youngest Svardian Princess?'

'It's a palace phone and the King of Svardia gave his permission,' Lykos replied without betraying the direction of his thoughts.

'I know that, but what kind of brother hires *you* to track down a twenty-two-year-old princess?'

'What is that supposed to mean?' Lykos demanded.

'It means, *adelfe mou*, I know you.'

'She is a pampered princess in the midst of a temper tantrum, she's about as far from my type as possible,' Lykos growled, indignant at the thought.

'What are you getting out of it then?' Theron needled him, clearly aware that Lykos wouldn't be doing this out of the kindness of his heart. Even the thought of it was laughable. 'If this has anything to do with Kozlov—'

'Get back to your drywall, Theron, if that's what the kids are calling it these days,' he interrupted, forcing a levity into his tone he didn't feel in the slightest. It was disconcerting that Theron had identified why he was willing to kidnap a princess.

'Lykos—'

He hung up the phone before Theron could finish his sentence, knowing his fellow Greek wouldn't understand the need driving him. Lykos pulled at his cufflinks as he looked up at the four-star Paris hotel where Princess Marit of Svardia intended to get married in little less than half an hour.

'No amount of dressing up will erase the fact that you are, and always will be, nothing more than a street thief unwanted even by your parents, left to scrabble around for scraps.'

The unwelcome memory of Ilian Kozlov's words sliced Lykos's focus in two. He'd come across the Russian when competing for controlling shares in a tech company three years ago. But besting the 'businessman' only seemed to inflame the elitist snob. Kozlov had started to come after Lykos's portfolio and when that hadn't worked he had crossed the line by impugning Lykos's reputation. And why? Because Lykos was a threat. He was one of the few men in the world with enough financial acumen and backing to take Kozlov down.

So now Kozlov would have to pay. Personally.

The King of Svardia had finally agreed to sell him the shares Lykos needed to oust Kozlov from his own company. That was, Lykos had decided, the price to be exacted for the Russian's insult. And all Lykos had to do? Be the thief that Kozlov had accused him of being and steal a princess.

As he entered the hotel, Lykos thought of what he'd read in Theron's file on André Du Sault. He had enough money in the bank account so generously provided by his rich parents that he could have taken Princess Marit anywhere. The hotel, Lykos supposed as he marched straight past reception as if he were a guest with every right to be there, was quaint. Charming, he'd imagine it being described... but definitely below André's means.

Lykos added a little more steel to his determination. That was not how to treat a woman. Even if that woman was a spoilt princess who had run away with some university crush. He took the steps of the elegantly curved staircase to where Lykos guessed her suite would be, continuing until he reached the top floor.

'Monsieur?'

Lykos refused to acknowledge the hotel porter he passed in the corridor.

'*Monsieur!*'

His eyes narrowed on the suite at the very end of the hall.

'*Monsieur, arrêtez!* Wait, *monsieur*! You cannot go in there. *Monsieur!*'

Lykos's fingers wrapped around the handle of the door and pushed. Standing in front of a mirror in a dress that did absolutely nothing for her figure or colouring was Princess Marit of Svardia. And still she was the most beautiful woman he'd ever seen.

It was a moment of pure shock, the realisation turning him to stone. In the space of a single heartbeat he'd taken in everything about her. Blonde hair in angular waves made him think of the way the surf hit the beach at Piraeus. Slashes of crimson across her cheeks, harsh and bright against the pallor of her skin. Eyes, large orbs of hazel with flecks of gold and jade so bright he could see them from across the room. Her mouth, part opened in shock, was somehow the most erotic thing he'd seen in a lifetime of debauchery. He had caught her mid-turn, swamped by tulle, her waist seeming so small he'd be able to cradle it in his hands. But it was the scattering of freckles across her nose that drew him up short, their presence speaking of an innocence he should steer well clear of.

Lykos bit back a curse. Marit was barely twenty-two years old and he ruthlessly marshalled his body's shocking reaction to her with a severity that was near painful. By the time he'd controlled his startling response he looked up to find that golden flecks had transformed into hissing sparks.

Oh, she was *mad*.

Marit turned fully, kicking the skirts out of her way as she did so, fury and fear mixing potently in her blood.

'I take it my brother sent you?' she asked. But trying to contain the seething anger only made her sound imperious and she internally cringed as she thought she saw a curl of distaste pull at the man's lip.

'He would like you to return to Svardia.' His accent made her think of salt and money, strangely.

Instinctively she took a step back. 'I have every intention of doing so, but first—'

'*Un*wed,' the man all but growled, taking a single step towards her, returning the distance to what it had been.

Fire scorched her. *No*. She couldn't return to Svardia until she was married. If she was not, then Aleksander would have to choose a husband for her. A stranger. And she couldn't let that happen.

'No.'

'Yes.'

'I can imagine it easily escaped the notice of one of my brother's minions—'

'*Minion*,' the man repeated as if it were some great insult.

'But this is the twenty-first century and—'

Her words were cut short the moment he swept

into the room, stalking towards her in such a way
that had her stepping back again, or at least trying
to. Her heel tangled in the hundredth layer of tulle
and, swaying dangerously on the other, she was about
to go down when the man appeared before her, bent
down and, to Princess Marit of Svardia's utter shock,
hoisted her over his shoulder.

'What on earth do you think you are doing?' she
cried as her hands scrabbled down his back, desperate for something to hold onto as he bent again to
pick up her bag and hook it over his other shoulder.
She lifted her head, shaking strands of hair from her
vision, trying to ignore the itch across her cheeks
from the rush of blood to her head, and cried out for
André. As they entered the corridor his door swung
open and her fiancé rushed out to a stop.

'André! Please—' Her words were cut off by
a wave of nausea as the man carrying her swung
around, presumably to face her fiancé. Holding her
breath, Marit strained her ears for the words André
would surely say in order to rescue her from her
captor.

One second, two.

Nothing.

Her heart sank as the man swung back to continue towards the staircase. Blinking back the mois-
ture in her eyes, she glared at André, who refused
to meet her gaze, a miserably mouthed apology on
his lips. She clenched her jaw and tried not to think
unkindly of the friend who had at least in some way
tried to help her. It wasn't André's fault. It was her

brother's. And the man carrying her over his shoulder like a…like a…

She growled. Actually growled. Anger caused her to lash out and pummel his back with her fists. Without even a pause in his stride, he flexed his back one way then the other, throwing her a little closer into the crook of his neck, the muscles across his shoulders and back rippling through the tulle and cotton of their clothes, whispering of a power that did shocking things to her core.

'Thank you, *glykiá mou*, I've been meaning to get a massage for some time now.'

Growling again, she tried to lever herself upright to respond when she felt his palm come down firmly against her backside, holding her in place.

'Stop it, Princess, or you'll fall off. And you're not a package that has insurance if it breaks.'

His words should have made her blush with anger. But that wasn't what had brought heat to Marit's cheeks or an ache between her legs. Embarrassed at the things she was feeling just from the hand holding her in place, Marit barely saw the bellboy who had brought the wedding dress to her suite only an hour ago.

'Your Highness?' He stared at her, shock clear on his face. 'Wait!'

Marit was surprised when the man beneath her stopped and turned.

'Who are you and what are you doing with Princess Marit?' the young bellboy asked, his voice trembling but determined. He couldn't be more than nineteen at the most, only a few years younger than her, but certainly many more years younger than the man carrying her over his shoulder.

She felt the subtle lean in the man's head, as if he were assessing the bellboy, and he grunted as if respecting the teenager for challenging him.

'Lykos Livas. Call this number,' he said, passing the bellboy a card from his pocket. 'If you are not satisfied, call the police.'

Lykos. A strange name, Marit thought. Greek, perhaps? *Wolf.* She thought of silver eyes and the power that arced through his torso as he moved, the lithe, easy grace of him. Yes. It was a name that suited him well.

'How do I know you are who you say you are?' she heard the bellboy ask, unable to see their interaction. But she most definitely felt the smirk of arrogance shiver through Lykos seconds before his answer.

'Google.'

Lykos turned on his heel and stalked from the building—the bellboy's interruption restoring his faith in humanity just a little. What kind of world was it that allowed a woman to be taken from her hotel room without her permission by a complete stranger, without a single person stopping them?

That he was the man doing the taking was neither here nor there. It was an outrage.

He adjusted his hold on the Princess over his shoulder, pulling the car keys from his pocket with his free hand, and clicked the button that released the locks. He went round to the passenger side, ignoring the wide-eyed looks from Parisian pedestrians, opened the door, threw the tote bag in first and then poured the Princess into the seat.

As he went to close the door he heard an angry voice demand that he 'watch the dress' from somewhere in the middle of all the...froth. Rolling his eyes, he swept up as many of the layers as he could, pressed them awkwardly into what little space remained and carefully closed the door. He returned to the driver's side and just as he reached for the handle a delicate wrist flicked out from amongst the masses of tulle filling the car and pressed down the lock.

'Really?' he demanded, flicking the lock on the keys.

And just as quickly she pressed the lock down again.

'Seriously?' he said, patience wearing thin.

'Seriously,' she said in that little half growl of hers that reminded him more of a kitten than a lion.

Turning his back to the window, he pinched the bridge of his nose. If Theron could see him now, he'd be in tears. Actual tears.

Lykos pivoted back to face the car. He couldn't see her through the layers of dress froth, but he'd expect her to be watching him closely. He pressed the key fob again for good measure and, as expected, she pressed down against the internal lock.

He looked up. 'Officer,' he said, shock marking

his features, his hands raised in surrender. 'It's not what it looks like…'

He saw movement amongst the masses of material, hit the key fob and pulled the door before she could realise it had been a ruse, sliding into the driver's seat and slamming the door behind him.

'Officer! Officer!'

'Sorry, Princess. No police officer.'

'What? No!' The bridal dress shifted again, hands pressing the skirts down to reveal a mass of blonde hair that looked less bed head and more utter mess and two hazel eyes that bored holes into what little conscience Lykos had left. He shrugged it off and fired the car's ignition, the purr of the engine easing his irritation and putting him firmly back in control.

Before he put the car into gear, he turned to those hazel eyes still spitting fire. 'I know you've thought about it, but I'll ask you not to mess with the car while I'm driving. It's dangerous and you'll hurt yourself. Or worse, me. Your brother told me you were reckless, but not stupid. I'm counting on that.'

The cupid's bow thinned and her cheeks flushed, which only made the scattering of freckles across her nose and cheeks more prominent. He flexed his fingers around the steering wheel and took her silence for surrender. He nodded, satisfied, and pulled away from *Le Jardin Exquis*.

Driving in Paris was a lot like driving in Athens: crazy, stupid and the most fun Lykos had had in ages. The beeped horns, the curses, the raised fists. It forced him to focus on the restrained chaos of the roads rather than his feelings as he tried to ignore the push of his need for vengeance and the pull of the woman in a wedding dress beside him. Twenty minutes later he pulled into the underground parking beneath his apartment that was about as far from Athens as he could get, and turned off the engine.

'What happens now?' The question came from the powder puff beside him, but the tone scratched against his conscience.

'We call your brother and arrange for you to be sent home.'

He saw the hand closest to him, slender and pale, form a fist that looked delicate more than dangerous. He could practically feel her need to rebel. To argue. But she had to know by now that it would be useless.

'Do we have a truce?'

There was silence. Eventually the tulle rustled as if she had nodded. Lykos exited the car and waited. But nothing happened. With a great deal of suppressed impatience, he walked around to the passenger side and opened her door for her. A silver-shod foot thrust from the skirts at the same time as a hand, which he reached for only because Lykos honestly couldn't see another way of her getting out of the car. But tugging gently on the hand brought her out and much closer than he had ever intended.

Large eyes stared up at him, shards of jade slicing through rich caramel, framed by long thick lashes. His gaze dropped to her lips, slick with gloss, but the cherry-red richness was all natural. The sheer vitality of her struck a note within him and vibrated into a chord of need that wound out from the deepest core of his being.

Until he remembered who she was. And who he was.

Marit's breath puffed from her chest into the space between them the moment the look in his eyes changed. Before then she'd felt... She shook her head. She'd felt nothing more than stress from the day's events.

But it had been the first time she'd been able to properly look at the man who had kidnapped her. His eyes were the palest grey, which was why she'd thought them silver earlier. His brow was low and made him look frustrated. Or it was simply the effect she had on him. High cheekbones cut into an angular face not softened by the swirls of artfully trimmed dark hair covering his jaw. He was taller than her by quite a bit and she felt tiny. As if everything about him surrounded and dwarfed her and for a moment it had been...delicious.

Until ice had formed in those silvery depths and she had to resist the urge to shiver. She cast her eyes over his shoulder to the exit sign. Maybe she could—

'Don't even think about it,' he commanded as his hand wrapped around her bicep and he guided her to a bank of lifts at the back of the car park.

They watched in silence as the lights counted down the floors and when the lift doors opened she couldn't tell who was more surprised, she and Lykos or the elderly couple disembarking.

'My child, are you okay?' The look of concern was unmissable across the woman's heavily wrinkled face.

The question pulled Marit up short. No one had asked her that since she'd been told she would be needed as second in line to the throne. No one had asked her that, even though her entire life was about to change, even though she'd never be able to continue with her youth project, given her new royal obligations, even though she would never be just *Marit* again. The empathy shining in the warm brown eyes knocked a chink into her armour and for a second she thought she might cry.

Until she was roughly tugged against the side of Lykos's lean torso, knocking the air out of her lungs.

'Oh, it's so very sad,' Lykos said, shaking his head and tutting as he pushed Marit into the lift. 'Jilted at the altar.' The gasps of shock from the couple were just too much. Marit gritted her teeth as he swiped his card in front of the scanner for the penthouse suite. 'I blame the dress, personally,' he pronounced as the lift doors closed.

CHAPTER TWO

How dared he?

Marit knew that it was the height of ridiculousness to be mad at Lykos for—of all things—his comment about a dress she knew did absolutely nothing for her shape or colouring, but somehow that sent fire coursing through her bloodstream.

It was her wedding dress! Or at least it would have been if he hadn't shown up, hoicked her over his shoulder and kidnapped her. For the rather long ride in the lift to the penthouse suite she fumed, getting more and more angry as Lykos appeared less and less bothered.

No. Worse, he seemed to positively *enjoy* her ire.

Lykos moved with the doors as they opened, stepping directly into an apartment that was instantly and obviously breathtaking. Over the years Marit had visited some incredible places with her family on their diplomatic tours, but there was a sleek sophistication to this space that spoke specifically of the male beside her.

'You live here,' she realised as she watched him

visibly adjust into the space. On any other man it might have looked as if he were relaxing into it, but there was nothing relaxed about the lines of tension in his body as he pulled sharply at each of his cufflinks.

'Sometimes,' he threw over his shoulder as he went towards a discreet but clearly well stocked bar. While his response didn't tell her much about the strange sarcastic Greek, the apartment spoke volumes.

Arrogant. Rich. Male. It screamed from every single thing she could see.

'You're not one of my brother's men, are you?' she asked as the suspicion that she knew what was going on began to evaporate like steam from a coffee cup. This man, this *Lykos Livas*, was absolutely nothing like the security service men she knew from Svardia.

'No.' The single word held such a significant amount of hubris she was distracted by the sheer arrogance of it, until she realised what he'd said.

Fear turned in her stomach, forcing threatening thoughts through her mind. Had her brother even sent him? Had she just been kidnapped by some shady foreign enterprise hoping to cash in on her brother's new ascension to the throne? Her fingers fisted into her palms as she scanned the room for exits.

As if he'd noticed the turn in her thoughts, he sighed. 'You wait until I have you out of your hotel, off the streets and in my apartment and *now* you panic?'

Although the tone of his voice clearly showed how unimpressed he was with her self-preservation skills, he hadn't heard her scream yet and she was just about to open her mouth to do so when—

'Adagio.'

'What?' Marit demanded.

'Aleksander told me your safe word,' he said, waving his hand dismissively. 'Adagio. The name of your pet hamster when you were five. Something about it being ironic because he was fast?' The tall, dark-haired man shook his head as if bemused at the words coming from his own mouth. 'Your safe word,' he repeated, as if speaking to a child. 'So that you know he sent me for you.'

Marit closed her mouth but continued to glare at him until she worked out what he was saying. Only her brother and the close protection officers in the Svardian security services knew of her safe word. But then it was possible that someone in the SSS had sold that information. But why would someone use *her* to blackmail the King of Svardia? Unless they had discovered the truth about Freya...

'Okay, stop. I can hear your mind whirring from here.' Lykos sighed. 'Here.' He passed her his phone.

It was a video file, her brother's face paused at the beginning. She hit play, noticing that the phone was warm from where Lykos had held it.

'Marit, I trust Lykos. You can too. He will bring you back home and we will straighten this all out. For now, just stay put. And don't marry anyone!'

Marit felt awful, hating to see the dark smudges

beneath her brother's eyes. He looked exhausted and, although his words had been half joking, there'd been a deep frustration that spoke of the weight of a new crown and the fear for his younger siblings. Marit clenched her jaw as shame drove nausea from her stomach.

All Aleksander was trying to do was ensure that Freya was protected. The fact that Marit might even be interfering with that was anathema to her. She really wasn't trying to cause problems for Aleksander, and certainly not Freya. Her brother would rule Svardia fairly and proudly and, even though he might have lost all sense of fun and joy in his late teenage years, he would do the best for their country. Always. It was just that…she had wanted to go into her new royal role with someone by her side. Someone there just for her. And that was now impossible.

She nodded, passing the phone back to Lykos, hating that he'd seen the video and despairing of what he saw when he looked at her. A runaway princess, spoiled and a royal pain. She couldn't meet his gaze so, instead, let herself be drawn to windows that looked out on an artfully designed rooftop terrace that surveyed Paris in a proprietorial way.

It was over. There was nothing left to do now but return to Svardia. That thought changed her heartbeat from two-four time to four-four, doubling in speed. What on earth did she know about the royal duties her older sister so effortlessly performed? She was grace and sophistication, where Marit was stiff and awkward. She always said the wrong thing under pressure and the only time she felt even remotely like the way Freya looked when she was performing royal duties was when she played the piano. How on earth would she survive, knowing that she could never measure up to her sister? That her family—most especially her parents—would always compare them and find her wanting.

The hiss of a machine and the scent of coffee drew her attention back to the man who would return her to all of that.

'How do you know my brother?' she asked, even now trying to put off thoughts of the future.

'Investments,' he replied, his voice moving behind her as she peered through the glass, beyond the large rust-effect metal containers displaying large green palm fronds, to the firepit and a single chaise longue that was large enough for two, sending wicked thoughts into her mind in an instant. Inside was no better. She glanced from wall to wall, every single furnishing was lush and textural: leather, fur, satin overlaid mahogany and black metal in every neutral colour imaginable.

Tactile.

The word came from the décor, not the man himself, she insisted mentally. And then she remembered the feel of his hand on her—

'Coffee?'

'Yes,' she answered too quickly.

Lykos resisted the urge to shake his head. How on earth had this woman been able to commit so much trouble when she had the world's worst poker face? Her gaze flickered from the coffee in his hand to the window, to the doors of the lift, until it rested beneath a frown, somewhere over his shoulder.

'Investments?' she queried.

'Yes.'

'With a sideline in kidnapping and extortion?'

'Where did you get extortion from?'

'I presume you're getting something in return?'

'Yes, Princess. In the real world that's called payment.'

Lykos clenched his jaw shut. He shouldn't have said that. He might not have a very high opinion of runaway princesses but that didn't excuse rudeness. He held out the coffee he'd made for her, waiting for her to meet his eye. He shouldn't have said it, but he wouldn't be shamed by it. And when she finally met his gaze steadily—going up a notch in his estimation—he wouldn't forget that Princess Marit of Svardia had absolutely no clue how the real world worked.

'I take mine—'

'Milk with two sugars?'

'How did you—?'

'Lucky guess,' he threw over his shoulder as he returned to make his own: black, bone-dry and unsweetened. How had he known? She was soft and pampered, that was how.

'So, what is the going rate for kidnapping a princess these days?'

'All your brother's shares in an oil company.'

A frown marred the smooth plane of Marit's brow

when he turned back to face her. 'What oil company?'

'Does it matter?'

She narrowed her eyes, watching him for a beat. 'It does to you,' she observed.

His heart thudded and Lykos realised he didn't like that she'd been able to see that so easily. Like Theron. He shrugged off his discomfort but a small smile pulled at the corner of her lips and his attention snagged on it. By the time his gaze flicked back to her eyes he couldn't help but feel that she'd done the same thing, as if he'd felt the brush of her eyes on his lips too.

'Kozlov Industries,' he answered, anchoring their conversation in something far too boring for a princess. Paradoxically, Marit shifted her skirts a little and proceeded to collapse into the seat in a froth of tulle, her cup held high through the dramatic move, and looked for all the world as if she were ready for a story.

'What does Kozlov Industries do?' she asked when he refused to give in to her unspoken command to explain further.

He glared at her, unsure as to why it was of any interest to her.

'What?' she asked with faux innocence. 'I just want to know what I'm worth to you, is that so bad?'

He didn't like the way she'd phrased that: '*what I'm worth to you*'. The words crawled beneath his skin and slithered through his memories until they churned in his gut.

'What you are *not* worth to me is the giant head-ache that's beginning to form.'

'All you have to do is answer the question,' she she childishly, 'and I'll leave you alone.'

'I doubt that very much,' he growled, pressing a finger to his temple and rubbing at the place where, genuinely, a headache was threatening to form. But when he looked back to where she was sitting in the chair like Little Miss Muffet—one of the only nurs-ery rhymes he remembered his mother whispering to him in the dead of night while his father was passed out—his mind emptied of excuses.

He knocked back his espresso, feeling the rich liquid burn his throat, before placing the cup back on the side. 'Kozlov is a Russian oligarch, with his fingers in far too many pies.'

Lykos thought of the man who he had first crossed paths with three years ago. The Russian thought nothing of buying up the competition and then break-ing the company apart, smashing it on the rocks and destroying hundreds and thousands of livelihoods. He was a man without conscience and as such was dangerous. Lykos had known plenty of bad men. Kozlov wasn't just *bad*, he enjoyed it, he relished the misery of others.

'You don't like him?'

Lykos barked out a bitter laugh. 'No, Princess. I don't like him.'

The man was a bully and a snob who had lashed out even harder when he'd realised that Lykos wasn't as easily toppled by snide rumours or business deals as he'd imagined. Lykos was slowly forcing him into a corner and the man was getting desperate. It had taken Lykos years of painstaking hard work to acquire even a small portion of shares in the man's company. Shell companies, clandestine meetings with CEOs on the brink of financial collapse who, with their last breath, threw their lot in with Lykos just to take revenge against the shark in the financial waters of the world's most vital stock exchanges. But Kozlov had finally realised what was happening and had blocked any attempts Lykos could make to further his shareholding in Kozlov Industries. Until he'd discovered the identity of a very surprising shareholder.

'Your brother, however, has shares in his flagship company.'

'How?'

'I believe there was a poker game involved.' Because Kozlov would *never* have sold anyone such a large stake in the company that was his shining triumph.

'My brother doesn't play poker,' Marit scoffed, as if the idea was farcical. But Lykos had seen with his own eyes just how good a poker player Svardia's new King was.

'I could be mistaken,' he replied in a tone that revealed he didn't think anything of the sort. 'Anyway, I return you to your brother unwed, and in exchange I get his shares in Kozlov Industries.' Those, combined with his own, would finally oust the oligarch from the company he'd founded.

The man's reputation would never recover.

'You want to take his company? Kozlov's?' she asked astutely. 'Why?'

He stalked towards the chair she was sitting in, placed his hands on the arms and leaned close enough to see the gold flecks in her eyes sparkle. 'Because he's a nasty man and I want to take it from him. That, Princess Marit, is all you need to know.'

This close, he could see the curve of her eyelashes, the soft freckles across her nose and cheeks and the way her lips sloped in a straight rather than curved line. They looked as if she'd been nibbling on the fleshy centre.

He pulled himself back, realising that he'd leaned in too far only by the way that the jade shards in her eyes flashed in warning.

Twenty-two. She was only twenty-two.

He turned away, disgusted with himself and the entire situation, spinning on his heel and leaving the room.

Marit blinked and blinked again, trying to clear the afterimage of Lykos left long after he'd gone. The determination that had marked his features as he'd warned her of his intent had been electrifying, but nothing compared to what it had morphed into.

Awareness. She'd felt it—his awareness of her as a woman—and her pulse hadn't recovered. She hadn't recovered. It was as if he'd reached out and touched her, and her heart had responded by trying to climb out of her chest.

And Lykos had seen that and left the room.

'Lykos?' she called, suddenly feeling a million shades of awkward.

'I'm calling your brother, then taking a shower,' she heard him shout from behind a door at the other end of the apartment.

No *make yourself at home*, no *help yourself to a drink or whatever you need. The toilets are here, here and here, and the exits are...* She turned back to the lift.

'And you need a key for the lift, which I have, so don't bother.'

She turned to glare in the direction the voice was coming from, but it didn't make her feel any better. She stood up and started to pace the living area, feeling a restlessness she didn't want to examine too closely. The idea of Lykos and her brother talking made her chest hurt and she rubbed her sternum a little to ease the tension there.

Aleksander would understand her actions, surely. He'd understand why she'd wanted to marry someone of her choosing. He *had* to. He'd known what it was like for her growing up. When they were younger Aleksander had, like Freya, tried to share some of their parents' attention with her but it had only made things worse. In her excitement, she'd become overeager, her actions too fast, causing her to spill something, or her words too quick, saying something nonsensical, irritating both her parents. After a while it became so painful for everyone, her siblings stopped and she gave up trying to impress them. Gave up trying to be seen. It had cut her off from the family unit, leaving her sticking out awkwardly at the side. And she'd promised herself never to feel that way again. Marit swallowed the emotions thickening her throat. If Lykos was on the phone with her brother, perhaps she should speak to him and at least get the shouting over and done with.

She followed Lykos's voice down a white-walled corridor to a rich walnut door at the end. It was slightly ajar and she could just make out what Lykos was saying.

'Yes, I know. But she's here now.'

'And André?' her brother's voice asked though the speaker of the phone.

Marit held back a little then, unable to resist, she peered through the crack in the door to see Lykos moving about what must be a bedroom beyond. He was in the process of removing his cufflinks.

'Won't be a problem.'

'You know this for sure?'

Lykos huffed out a laugh. 'Yes.'

Marit felt her cheeks colour with embarrassment at how easily André had let her go. He'd not even uttered a single word to stop Lykos. It hurt more than it should, digging into an older wound, a deeper one. She looked up to find Lykos shrugging out of his shirt and her breath caught in her lungs.

Her hand flew to her chest as her heart thudded against her ribs, while her eyes traced every single line and plane of Lykos's body. The muscles on display weren't puffed from excessive exercise but honed, earned, lithe and powerful. As if Lykos knew how to use what he had rather than just rely on brute force. Even his body hinted at a lethal intelligence that seemed to run contrary to the strange cynical sense of humour she'd seen him display. Broad shoulders tapered into thin hips, the dusting of hair across his pecs seemed a handspan to Marit, her fingers flexing outward as if to test her guesstimate.

'And Marit? How is she?' The concern in Aleksander's voice caught Marit by surprise. It was years since they had been anything that resembled 'close'. And his ascension to the throne in the last three months certainly hadn't helped that.

Her gaze returned to Lykos, who had stopped with his hands on his belt, frowning towards the phone as if unsure what to say. She flattened herself back against the corridor wall when his eyes turned towards the door, her pulse pounding in her throat.

'She is…fine,' Marit heard him say and the snap of leather told her he had removed his belt. Biting her lip, she was about to turn back to see if she could…

'Lykos, I need you to keep her.'

'What?'

What?

Lykos's voice had been as harsh and shocked as her own internal voice.

'Just for the week.'

'A week? Aleksander—'

'I will explain later.'

'I don't want her.' The explosive words cut into her like shrapnel.

'You would make a king beg.' It was less of a question from her brother, more of a statement.

'I will expect something very great in return,' she heard Lykos growl.

Nausea rose in Marit's stomach and the fingers that pressed against her lips shook.

He didn't want her here.

'I'll see to it that you have it.'

She turned to lean against the wall, her breaths short and puffy as she wilted down to the floor.

No one wanted her. Not unless they were paid for it.

It wasn't an unfamiliar feeling and she tried to tell herself that she should know this by now. She hadn't been the important sibling, she hadn't been taught the same things, treated the same way, wanted the same way. Loved. She had been unseen for so much of her life. Until now. And even now she wasn't really wanted. She was the only stand-in available. She was the worst-case scenario.

'What is it that you expect me to do with her for a week?'

'Just…keep her away from here and out of trouble.'

She bit her lip until a faint metallic taste hit her tongue. The sharp sting pulled her back to the present, her brother's words finally registering. He should have known better.

She heard Lykos sigh. 'She's a princess. How much trouble can she be?'

Poor man, Marit thought. He had no idea.

* * *

Water poured over Lykos's skin, the freezing jets raising goosebumps and thankfully not much else. He breathed through his nose, trying to calm the emotions swinging between resentment that he'd been lumbered with a spoilt princess, irritation that a brother would be so neglectful of his sister and frustration. Because that spoilt princess happened to be causing a reaction he'd not experienced since his teenage years.

He couldn't understand it. She was absolutely not his type. His preference leant towards brunettes that were his age or older, with sleek sophistication and absolutely no desire for a commitment he would never give. Marit was... He cursed. She was nearly ten years younger than him. The thought had him clenching his jaw. It didn't take a genius to work out that she was innocent too. The way she had looked up at him in the car park... There hadn't been an ounce of artifice about her or her reaction to him.

He shut off the water and turned for a towel before the memory of that moment could take hold of his body and lead to another twenty minutes in a freezing cold shower. He dried his body with harsh strokes, as if he could rid his skin of the desire to reach for her.

Stamáta!

Enough. He had more control over himself than this. Wrapping a towel around his waist, he strode into the bedroom and stopped immediately.

For his entire childhood he'd lived in a constant

state of hyperawareness. Firstly because of his father's fists and then at the orphanage, where fear and desperation were tools to be used against the weak. Consequently, he had a very specific alertness to his surroundings, especially his possessions, where they were and, most importantly, where they weren't. And he hadn't left his trousers on the bed. With his hand clutching the towel, he stalked through his apartment to confirm what he already knew.

She was gone.

The Princess's tote bag had been removed from where he had left it on the floor of the living area and in its place was a wedding dress. He skirted it as if it were a dangerous animal—which, to a man whose idea of hell was holy matrimony, it might as well have been. It looked as if she'd let the froth pool at her feet like champagne and simply stepped out of it. His imagination was suddenly a wild cascade of erotic images of toned limbs in silver heels and a waist he wanted to bracket with his hands.

None of which helped him with the fact that he had a princess on the loose in Paris and he needed to find her. Now. He marched back to his room, discarded the towel and dressed with the same ruthless efficiency he used to marshal his financial empire. The entire time he reassessed everything that he knew about the Princess. Reluctantly, he was forced to admit that he had written her off as nothing more than a spoilt princess with a rebellious streak. But while he accepted that he had been played, the game was not over and by the end she would realise that it was she who had underestimated the lengths he would go to secure his payment for her capture and containment.

He scanned his wardrobe and identified which items were missing: one pair of black superfine wool dress trousers, one white shirt and one thin black leather belt. Presumably the Princess was still wearing silver heels.

He pulled at his cuff sleeves, the snap of cotton familiar and satisfying. He reached for his cufflinks and threaded the fixed bar through the buttonhole, feeling his pulse settle with the familiar act and the air of respectability they lent him. He lifted the suit jacket that held his wallet from the back of the chair and stopped. The weight was off and he flung the jacket back on the seat and pinched the bridge of his nose.

Lykos couldn't believe it.

He, who had once been the most notorious pickpocket in Athens, had just had his wallet stolen.

By a princess.

CHAPTER THREE

MARIT LOOKED OUT of the back window of the taxi hurtling through Paris towards the Gare du Nord train station. She'd half-expected to see Lykos running out of the entrance of the swanky apartment building in nothing but a towel. But he hadn't.

Ignoring the strange pang of disappointment, she turned instead to riffle through the dark brown leather wallet she'd taken from Lykos's jacket pocket. The only reason she hadn't taken the car was because she didn't know how to drive, so she'd settled for throwing his car keys off the balcony, her only regret that she wouldn't be there to see the look on his face when he realised what she'd done.

The eyes of the taxi driver flickered over her through the rear-view mirror and she clenched her jaw. It was not as if she'd been spoilt for choice. She'd hardly have been able to make a quick getaway in the wedding dress. She'd rolled up the hems of the trousers and cinched the belt tightly around her waist beneath a shirt that definitely passed as oversized and had managed to appear almost stylish.

Marit counted eight hundred euros in cash, but no credit cards. Unusual, yet somehow fitting for a man she believed enjoyed being contrary for the sake of it. She looked into each little pocket. No photos, no receipts, nothing tucked away for safety. There was no sense of who he was. She pulled out a driver's licence and stared at the black and white image of Lykos Livas, frowning in all his brooding glory. How could she dislike someone so intensely, yet still feel acutely…acutely…*not* like the way any other man had ever made her feel?

She threw the wallet into the bag by her feet, catching sight of the bright red cover of her passport, which she needed to get into Italy. Unlike her brother and sister, the amount of freedom she'd enjoyed up until recently had meant that she'd been able to keep hold of it, rather than handing it over to close protection officers. Of course that would change when she took her sister's place in the royal family. Security details, every minute of her day planned to the second, public speaking, public events… Sweat started to gather at the back of her neck.

As the lights turned, allowing the taxi to move closer to the train station, her pulse picked up. The closer she came to her last bit of freedom, the more fearful she became that it would disappear. Images of a strong male hand wrapping around her bicep had her heart thrumming in her chest. Her breaths came quicker as she glanced at the sign for the Gare du Nord and she nearly cried when the taxi was caught in another stream of traffic. She glanced behind her again, in caser Lykos had somehow found her. No. She couldn't stay here. It was as if she could feel him snapping at her heels.

'*Arrêtez-vous ici, s'il vous plait,*' she said, and the driver pulled to the side of the road. She thrust twice the amount needed at the driver and launched herself from the cab. Pulling the tote over her shoulder, she jogged down the street towards the station. She checked the time. She had just over fifteen minutes to buy her tickets and get on the next train to Milan if she hurried.

She wondered whether Lykos would tell Aleksander what had happened, or whether he'd try to find her before he had to.

I need you to keep her.
Just for the week.
I don't want her.

The words ran on a loop through Marit's mind. It would serve Lykos right if Aleksander found out and decided not to give him the shares. She had half a mind to let her brother know of her escape, if she didn't think it would lead directly to her capture.

Drawing a few curious glances, she entered the train station and found the departures board. Checking the train was on time, she rushed over to the ticket stall. She wasn't running away. She *would* go back, just…not yet.

Her heart turned over as she thought of just how much Freya loved what she did, how good she was at it. A better princess hadn't been born. Marit had argued with her over and over again, insisting that Freya didn't need to step down, but she wasn't blind. The press were cruel and a princess with fertility issues… one who was supposed to provide spare heirs for a ruler so new and untested as their brother… Reporters would tear her apart and the fallout would cause deep fissures in the confidence of the Svardian people in their royal family. The international implications didn't bear thinking about.

So, no. Marit was under no illusions as to where her future lay. It was just that before she did step into Freya's shoes she wanted some time to herself. To do some of the things she'd thought she'd have the time to do, to feel all that she'd wanted to feel, and to experience all that she possibly could before her life became one of dictates and strangers and public royal duties…and marriage and children she wasn't ready for.

Her fingers drummed a beat against the cold steel of the ticket office counter as she waited for the clerk to process the cash payment and checked her watch. She had five minutes to get to her train before it left.

Lykos looked up at the train station sign. Why? His only explicable reason was that it was where he would have come. But he felt it deep in his gut—the part of him he'd learned to trust when he was young and on the streets. She was here. The problem now was figuring out where she was going to.

As he took stock, he pulled at the cufflinks, setting the shirt smartly beneath his jacket, and he cursed the Princess *again*. The first time he'd cursed was when he'd caught sight of the small key fob he'd wasted precious minutes looking for, fragmented into microchips and black plastic on the road outside the apartment, that would take time and money to replace. And if Lykos hated anything it was unnecessary waste, he thought as he revised his earlier impression of Marit once again. Definitely spoilt and completely ignorant of the value of money or possessions.

As he entered the sprawling international train station, the sound of thousands of voices filled the air and Lykos began to feel the first stirrings of unease. A childhood habit rose from the mists of time to snake around him as he instinctively scanned the sea of people for targets—just like his father had taught him. And he saw them all. The wealthy businessman making a show of checking his expensive watch to the girl at the kiosk counter. The man rolling his eyes as his wife debated which magazine would be best for her trip. The mother in expensive clothes, telling off her teenage son while her daughter made faces at the boy behind her mother's back.

Lykos rolled his shoulders, trying to shake off the discomfort the instinctive act made him feel. As a seven-year-old, he'd have had three fat wallets within fifteen minutes and a hard smack across the cheek for leaving the easiest prey of all. The grey-haired lady with the walking frame, her bag hanging half open from the handle, picking through her open clasp wallet for change as if each penny was precious.

He glanced up at the departures board. London,

Brussels, Belgium, Germany, Milan, the Netherlands. Of course, if it were him, he'd have been tempted to disappear into the underground and stay in Paris. But while he was sneaky, Marit was rebellious. And they were two very different things. Surely a young, rebellious woman wouldn't be able to resist the lure of London. He checked the time and the platform number. Ten minutes. Easy.

He passed the stall with the irritated mother and the lecherous businessman, and found his target. He stood directly in her line of sight.

'*Mademoiselle?*'

'*À mon âge?*' the elderly lady replied with a twinkle in her eyes, her hands shaking so that he worried for the contents of her purse.

Lykos nodded. '*Madam,*' he corrected with a small bow of his head. '*Je peux?*' he asked, tucking the fallen strap of her bag securely over the handle bar of her walking frame without her notice.

'*Mais oui. Merci.*'

The businessman scowled at him and the girl at the kiosk counter's eyes followed Lykos as he stalked off to the train to London, *after* buying the elderly lady's magazine.

Marit found her window seat on the quiet train, casting looks up and down the carriage, still convinced the enigmatic Greek would come stalking down the train to snatch her back up. The overhead announcement warned passengers they had one minute before departure.

Her heart pounding in her chest, Marit slid into the window seat, putting her bag on the seat between her and the aisle, hoping that it would deter a stranger from taking it. She held her breath as she heard the beeps sounding that the train doors were closing. Her eyes drifted shut and she prayed.

Please. Just give me this. Then I'll do what's needed, I promise. Just this.

Her heart lurched forward with the sudden jerk of the TGV, adrenaline coursing through her veins along with a sense of victory. She had a feeling that fooling Lykos Livas wasn't an everyday occurrence.

But now that the train was moving she allowed herself to think about her destination when she arrived in Milan. She reached into her bag for her music player, fitting the wireless pods into her ears and pressing play, letting the opening notes from one of her favourite songs slide over her, familiar and soothing.

She'd wanted to visit Sforzando for years, its reputation as the best blues bar in Italy unprecedented. Marit might have been given many freedoms over the years, but there were some her parents had still baulked at.

Don't be silly, Marit. A princess can't be seen in a blues club.

Piano lessons are fine, as long as you stick to classical pieces. But a guitar is out of the question.

A music degree, Marit? Really? Don't be so naïve.

Fresh blooms of hurt sprang from the remembered words. What her parents—and even her siblings—

had failed to understand was that it wasn't just music, it wasn't just part of some rebellion. It was so much more than that. Music had been her escape. It was a way for her to express emotions and feelings that she was unable to put to words. It had been an outlet for her anger before she'd known it was anger, loss before she'd realised she'd felt loss, and an expression of yearning before she'd ever known what she was looking for.

She looked out of the window, unseeing of the bricks and wires twisting in the shadows as the train left the station to the sound of a deep, constant, rhythmic guitar strum that was hypnotic. She frowned when she felt a presence standing in the aisle on the other side of the seat where her bag was. More than a little disgruntled that the fellow passenger couldn't find any other seat to pick, she lifted her back and angled herself further away from the person, ignoring the way the man folded himself into the seat. Impossibly long legs looked almost comical pressed up against the back of the seat in front.

Just as her favourite singer proclaimed that she couldn't find her way home, a stillness settled in the air between her and the passenger, Marit's whole body filling with sudden tension as she slowly turned to find Lykos staring at her with a raised eyebrow.

Dammit!

She pulled the pod from her ear and he was momentarily distracted by the blush of anger forming on her cheeks, making those freckles even more golden.

'Hello, Princess,' said Lykos, leaning back against the seat, making a big show of getting comfortable, despite the way his pulse was racing from having to sprint to the train before it left. If he hadn't caught sight of the particular shade of blonde of Marit's hair from the corner of his eye as he took the escalators in the wrong direction he'd have completely missed her.

From the Princess's scowl, she clearly didn't realise how close she'd come to getting away with her plan, whatever that plan was. He shifted his shoulders, disliking the way that sweat stuck his shirt uncomfortably to his back, even as the youth in him delighted in the game, celebrated victory at having caught the Princess. It added a little flavour to the pounding of his heart in his chest.

'How did you find me?' she demanded.

'I'm that good.'

She narrowed her eyes. 'You got lucky.'

It was an accusation that had been levelled at him again and again over the years. At least one of them had been delivered in a Russian accent. But each and every one of them had been an underestimation of the determination and power driving him forward; of the lengths he would go to, to leave the dirt of the streets of Athens behind him. Had *left* behind him, he mentally corrected.

'Luck is what you make of it.' His father's words were out of his mouth before he could pull them back, leaving teeth marks on his tongue and burns deep in his heart. As if the verbal slip disproved his assertion that he was no longer the same street thief *scrabbling for scraps.* The sweat on his skin turned frigid and he wanted a shower to wash off the memories. Instead, he was leaving his apartment in Paris far behind him at a rate of knots.

'Why did you run?' he asked, rooting himself in the present. 'We had a truce,' he accused, the gravel in his voice vibrating from the distaste of a broken agreement.

'Clearly, I have some…*free time*…before I am needed in Svardia. I thought I'd do a bit of travelling.'

Christé mou, she'd overheard his conversation with Aleksander. And must have heard what he'd said after.

I don't want her.

It might have been the absolute truth in that moment, but the reality was always more complex. And, no matter the reason, no woman, no *one*, ever wanted to hear those words. Justifiable guilt swirled in a conscience he would have professed not to have.

But, Lykos realised, instead of falling into tears or retreating, the girl beside him had taken his clothes, stolen his wallet, destroyed his means of transport and got herself on a train to Milan. He was almost impressed.

He glanced at her from the corner of his eye. Her head was turned towards the window, the waterfall of golden hair tucked behind her ear, revealing the pod and the gentle hum of music he couldn't quite make out. The curve of her cheek was plumper than those high cheekbones of the brunettes he usually acquainted himself with. It spoke of a softness that belied the fire within her and he appreciated the duality, the drive, even if it came at his expense. An expense that he couldn't afford. Kozlov needed to pay and Aleksander had the shares to help make it happen.

Lykos felt her shiver, as if Marit had somehow picked up on the sudden drop in temperature from his thoughts alone. He frowned, realising the closeness of the seats. 'Why did you not buy a first-class ticket?'

Catching her gaze in the reflection on the glass, he marshalled the jolt that continued to shock his body, until she broke the connection.

'I wanted to save the money,' she said with a shrug.

'What would a princess know about saving money?' Lykos scoffed, remembering in a heartbeat every single time he'd scrabbled in the street for pennies or, in desperation, used the 'skills' his father had taught him almost as soon as he could walk.

'Quite a lot, if she's never had free access to it herself.' She turned to look at him, her pupils flaring unconsciously as she registered how close they were; her body's response starting a chain reaction in his own, shorting out his ability to reply to her statement. 'What?' she asked of his silence. 'You think it's easy for a princess to go and get a summer job?' she demanded, clearly—and thankfully—misunderstanding the reason behind his lack of response. 'You ever wondered why royals don't have handbags? Because their wallets and keys are kept by security personnel. Why aren't I travelling first-class? Because the only money

I have is the money I took from your wallet. I was saving the rest for...'

Like a bloodhound, he followed the trail of unspoken words. 'For what, Princess?'

'My name,' she growled, 'is Marit. And clothes, of course. What else would I spend your money on?'

He stared at her, trying to see though the lie she'd told him, but he recognised the stubborn glint gleaming back at him. What he didn't recognise was the sense of kinship that suddenly bloomed in that moment. Because he realised she was protecting herself. And that Lykos both respected and understood. Neither of which would matter, of course, if it stopped him from getting what he was owed from Aleksander.

He turned away from her steady gaze, giving a point to the Princess, just as he heard her stomach growl and he allowed a smirk to pull at his lips, covering the strange sensation from seconds earlier.

'You see,' he drawled, 'if we were in first-class lunch would have been served by—'

She shot out a hand and slapped him on the arm.

'That's assault,' he warned mockingly, his head dipping slightly, only to be hit by a gentle hint of salt and the sweet scent of pears.

'It's self-defence. I'm being kidnapped,' she replied, and the breathless way the words escaped her lips hitched his pulse, causing an alarm to scream in his head.

'Actually, you ran away, so it's probably more akin to retrieval,' he couldn't help but reply.

'Retrieval?'

'And theft. You stole my wallet, my clothes, and I haven't even started on the car.'

'Did you find the keys?' she asked suddenly, the urgency and concern across her features startling. It was on the tip of his tongue to ask why she would care, when it hit him that, why aside, she did actually care.

'Yes, all fine,' he replied, fascinated by the concern leaving her features.

'It would have served you right if they hadn't been,' she chided.

'Yes, it would have,' he agreed, wondering why on earth he'd just spared her feelings. 'I'm going to hunt down some breakfast,' he said, easing himself out of his seat and into the aisle. 'Princess—'

'Marit.'

'*Marit.* Don't. Go. Anywhere.'

Her name, spoken in his thick, luscious accent, had struck her so still he needn't have warned her not to leave. Her body remained motionless long after he'd left the carriage until, unable not to, her lungs exploded into action with a huge inhale. She still felt pinpricks across her skin from how close he'd been, the way her heart had lurched as he'd teased her, the way each and every breath took in that rich, savoury scent of his aftershave, and the way she'd had to fist her hands to stop herself reaching for him.

Breathy. She'd sounded breathy, even to her own ears.

I don't want her.

Shame curled her stomach. Was she doomed to repeat this cycle over and over and over again, wanting people who didn't want her? The memory of nine-year-old Freya's face, when at the age of five Marit had asked if there was something wrong with her that she wasn't allowed to go to lessons with Mummy and Daddy rose in her mind anew.

A belief that had become more and more certain as the years had gone on. She didn't know why it was, only that it was. Her parents were not outwardly loving in any real way, unless there were cameras present, but even then she just wasn't as important as Freya and Aleksander were. Or at least she hadn't been until now.

Now, she was needed but still not wanted.

Marit's mouth trembled until she pressed her teeth together hard enough to make it stop. She couldn't forget that. Whatever had come over her, she had to remember where she was and who he was. Lykos Livas was acting on her brother's behalf and only then because he needed Aleksander's shares. He was not here for her.

By the time Lykos returned to his seat, Marit was putting all her efforts into focusing on the music rather than the man beside her. But even then, while the right side of her brain homed in on the notes and composition of the piece, the left side insisted on memorising everything about the Greek billionaire next to her.

Billionaire? Oh, absolutely. It wasn't the clearly expensive watch or the cut of his clothes that years as a princess had enabled her to recognise as hand-made, it was his attitude: a careless irreverence that she'd not encountered before amongst the courtiers at the Svardian palace or the international delegates, or even the students at the Swiss university her parents had made her attend.

He put down her tray table and placed on it a steaming paper cup of coffee and a slightly greasy paper bag and ignored her as studiously as she ignored him. She stared at the items he had procured and felt strangely as if she were being assessed as he consumed his pastry in impossibly large, man-sized mouthfuls. She felt the dare to refuse such simple food buzz against her skin as if the force of his thoughts pressed against her. Lykos was a man just as arrogantly comfortable at the coffee cart of the TGV as he was in a five-star hotel, which was most definitely at odds with the moneyed men and women she'd met throughout her life.

And, with that, she realised that she'd never met anyone like Lykos Livas.

Everything in her wanted to rebel, to refuse the food he'd bought simply from habit. But he clearly thought her too pampered a princess to stoop to the greasy offering, and that she rebelled against more. She turned to face him, reaching blindly for the flaky pastry inside, tore off as big a chunk as she possibly could, tipped her head back and fitted as much of it into her mouth as she could. She kept her eyes on his so she saw just how hard he was trying not to smile as he ate his own piece of pastry.

'You look ridiculous,' he dismissed, but the way the corner of his lips twisted hit her heart hard. Making him smile against his will? One of the best things about that day so far. Especially as she had the impression it didn't happen very often.

'It's really tasty,' she said with her mouth full, flakes of iced toasted almonds peppering her stolen shirt.

'Shut up and eat your breakfast.'

'It's three in the afternoon!'

'A croissant is *always* breakfast,' he replied imperiously, forcing her to choke back a laugh.

The next few hours were strange for Marit. It had started when he'd asked her about a castle.

'But you have one, yes?'

'Well, there *are* castles that belong to the royal family,' she'd tried to explain.

'Any for sale?'

'No, Lykos, none for sale,' she'd replied.

He'd seemed strangely disappointed and, after making a cryptic comment about always having wanted a castle, he'd simply leaned his head back against the headrest and settled. At one point his eyes had drifted shut.

She wasn't sure he was actually asleep, there was something alert about him—as if half of his mind was utterly aware of everything going on around him. Nevertheless, she took the time to study him. There was a small scar just beneath the corner of his mouth, glinting like a silvery line from the dark stubble, that marred his almost perfect jaw. His cupid's bow was so pronounced she wanted to press the pad of her thumb to the cleft above it. Lips carelessly sensual, thick and—she bit her bottom lip, mirroring her unconscious thoughts. His nose would have been straight as an arrow were it not for the slight kink near the bridge that made her think of fists and fights. His face whispered a history that seemed contrary to every wealthy person she'd ever known. He was a curiosity she needed to ignore, she decided as she skipped the next track on her playlist and looked out of the window at the Italian landscape.

'What's in Milan?'

She could pretend she hadn't heard him but that felt childish. She turned to find him looking at her as if waiting to navigate through her response for the truth and wondered what it would be like to just tell him, to give up this endless fight that she seemed to have been waging for years.

'There's a club I want to go to.' Because she was watching closely, she saw the glint of disappointment in his otherwise utterly impassive face. And it stung. 'Not that kind of club.'

This time his face blared mock innocence. 'What kind of club did you think I was—?'

'Not that kind of club either!' she scolded in a whisper, hating the way her cheeks pinked up at the sudden thought of Lykos in a…in a sex club. Her body started to tremble, low and strong, and for a moment she feared that Lykos could tell. As if he sensed her body's reaction because he went incredibly still, aside from the muscle at his jaw flexing as if he were bracing himself.

'What's in Milan, Marit?' he asked again, this time a strange force in his tone that she knew instinctively not to push.

'A blues club.'

This time, the look of surprise on Lykos's face looked genuine.

CHAPTER FOUR

LYKOS WONDERED WHEN he'd get a handle on Princess
Marit of Svardia. At almost every turn, she did the
opposite of what he was expecting. From the moment
the train had pulled in to Milan and the closer and
closer they got to this, apparently, world-renowned
blues club, she hadn't stopped talking. Passion and
enthusiasm lit her features as she named supposedly
famous musicians that had played in the hallowed
halls of Sforzando which she found 'inconceivable'
that he'd never heard of. Long gone was the pallor
he'd first seen across her features, or the frustrated
fury from his apartment in Paris. Blues and jazz, it
seemed, brought a bronze glow to her that vibrated
from her like sound waves, brushing against him
like the tide.

She was utterly lost in their conversation as they
walked the streets of Milan, unaware of the young
man who tripped over his feet at the sight of her,
or the woman who barged her boyfriend with her
shoulder for staring at Marit a little too long. Marit
seemed completely unaware of the effect she was

having—and Lykos knew that it was nothing to do with her title. In fact, from what he had gleaned, despite some rather painful and embarrassing encounters with the press as a young girl and teenager, all attention-seeking behaviour had seemed to stop after the skiing accident she'd had at fourteen. The resulting surgery had impacted her parents' diplomatic visit to Japan, Marit's mother returning to Svardia to take care of Marit while her father remained behind with his delegation.

Lykos had flicked through the press articles and photographs of Marit's mother descending the steps of a small jet, her face hollow with concern. She'd gone straight to the hospital, where more photographs caught her in intense discussions with doctors, appearing beside reports from the school friends on the same trip quoted as saying how scared they'd been and how reckless Marit had been.

Even now Lykos felt rising resentment at the childish behaviour of the young woman beside him. He would have given anything as a child to have his mother be with him when sick, instead of dropping him at an orphanage and not looking back even once.

Aleksander had briefed him on why he needed Marit to return to Svardia. He'd been sworn to secrecy over their sister's infertility issues that meant Marit needed to step up and into that role. And what had she done? Run away. And when Aleksander needed more time—the reason was honestly none of Lykos's business—she'd run away *again*. To a blues club.

With one ear he continued to listen to her expounding the virtues of different female singers in country blues and classic blues as he purposefully held onto his irritation. What he couldn't understand was why the knowledge of her spoilt selfishness was not enough of a deterrent to his body's reaction to her. Maybe he was coming down with something. A cold? The flu? It was inexplicable.

Lykos was acutely familiar with attraction and arousal. He was a healthy, virile Greek. He enjoyed his sexual exploits as much, if not more, than the next man. But blondes weren't his type. Princesses weren't his type. And twenty-two-year-olds who had absolutely no idea what they were doing were Not. His. Type.

He was so busy telling himself that, he hadn't realised that she'd stopped walking and pulled himself up short to find her staring up at a building ten feet behind him. The look on her face whipped concern through him in a heartbeat.

'Marit?' He closed the distance between them in short strides, the distress marring her features making him want to pull her to him. Her eyes sparkled with a sheen of tears she hastily tried to blink away. Teeth pierced her bottom lip, as if to stop it trembling. She swallowed once and then shrugged her shoulder.

'It's okay. It was foolish to come here without...' Marit's words trailed off as she looked back up at an old building that he could now see had once been a large three-storey bar. Chipboard covered all but a few windows, the rest shards of jagged glass. A sign that read 'Sforzando' was missing a few letters, old posters curled and peeled down from the wall, months if not years of rain and pollution destroying images of musicians and set lists. It reminded him of an old *rebetiko* tavern he and Theron used to sneak into when they were teenagers, but this building was derelict. No music played here any more.

He turned back to see Marit taking in the desolation of the building she had stolen a wallet and crossed countries to reach, and even if she was the spoilt youngest daughter of a king it didn't make her sadness any less real or evident.

'Marit,' he said, stretching out his hand.

She shook her head and stepped back from his reach, looking up and down the street to mask her feelings. She opened her mouth to speak, but the words wouldn't come and he realised that she'd come to the end of her fight, the defeat in her eyes so much worse than her rebellion or anger.

He whistled to the cab he saw turning into the top of the street and when it pulled up beside them he ushered Marit into the white car. Throughout the journey his gaze flickered back and forth between Marit, the road ahead and the driver who, thankfully, seemed to have no idea who his royal passenger was.

Lykos checked his watch. It was six-thirty by the time the driver pulled up outside the grand entrance of L'Aranceto. The liveried doorman had a frown on his face until the moment he recognised who it was emerging from the taxi.

'Signor Livas,' he said, walking forward with renewed vigour. 'My apologies, we weren't expecting you.'

'Nothing to apologise for, Benito. It was a spur-of-the-moment decision,' Lykos replied, reassuring the man with a friendly hand on his shoulder. 'Hence no luggage. Nevertheless, discretion would be appreciated,' he whispered congenially. Lykos didn't think that either Aleksander or Marit would appreciate a resurgence of rumours about Svardia's youngest royal, especially not now.

Benito dipped his head. 'Of course.'

Lykos turned back to the cab and held his hand out to Marit, who must have been upset as she took it without question or complaint. Which, perversely, Lykos didn't like one bit. It seemed as if she were in shock, but why it had been the blues club rather than—say—kidnap, a failed wedding or an international chase, Lykos honestly couldn't fathom.

He guided her through the gold-framed doors that Benito held open and nodded to him as he moved through to the hotel bar, knowing that the doorman would attend to checking them into suitable accommodation.

Over the years Lykos had travelled the globe, the transient nature of his business suiting his needs and his temperament, but this was one of his favourite hotels. The suites all had a balcony, which was necessary for a man who never slept well at the best of times but it was much worse when he couldn't see the sky, and the staff here knew him and liked him.

As evidenced by the smile he was greeted with from Oriana, the dark-haired beauty behind the bar who, despite being twenty years older, enjoyed their flirtatious banter as much as him.

'Lykos, it is very unkind of you to bring such a beautiful companion into my bar,' she chided, her English better than his Italian. Although a quirk of Lykos's intelligence had given him the ability to easily and quickly pick up foreign languages, he knew Oriana enjoyed the practice on a forgiving customer.

'If the situation wasn't so dire, I would never have betrayed you in such a way, *tesoro mio.*'

She flicked a white dishcloth at him that snapped satisfyingly through the quiet of the bar. 'Go sit down. I will bring you your drinks.'

'Grazie mille,' Lykos replied, a hand hovering at Marit's back, guiding her to a booth in the shadowed end of the bar.

Marit let him all but pour her into the seat at the round dark marble table and watched him with large eyes as he took his opposite her. He placed an elbow on the arm of his chair and leaned into his palm, rubbing the stubble on his chin as he watched her as openly as she watched him.

This time their connection wasn't one of challenge or judgement, rather it was a reassessment of sorts. So far, nothing in the last ten hours had been as he'd expected from the pampered Princess he'd read about in his file from Theron.

'You didn't order any drinks.'

'I didn't have to.'

'You're that good?' Marit asked with a raised eyebrow.

'No. Oriana is.'

Marit couldn't work him out. And she didn't like that. Although it was easier to focus on the enigmatic man in front of her than how she felt about Sforzando. She wished she could explain the longing she'd felt to visit the world-renowned blues club. The desire she'd had to see it before returning to Svardia so she could have a moment for herself to take back with her. to remember. to keep her going through the years of her duty.

The waitress placed two drinks down on the table between them. Lykos's was a dark amber swirl poured over a large ice cube in a short, square, heavy-looking glass, decorated with a twist of orange peel. Hers was a much lighter concoction, still orange, but served in a martini glass with a sprig of rosemary.

She felt Lykos's eyes remain on her the entire time the waitress was there, cutting through her natural instinct to rebel. That same yearning need she couldn't explain about Sforzando seemed to bleed onto Lykos. A yearning need for him to see her as she was and not as some spoilt runaway princess.

'How long do I have?' she asked. 'Before you return me to Svardia,' she clarified in response to the rise of his brow in silent enquiry.

'Five days.'

She bit her lip. 'Did he tell you why I'm needed back home?' she asked.

He nodded, his face half hidden in the shadows of the bar. But not well enough to hide the judgement, the distaste, at what he clearly saw was her running away. He didn't understand. She could—*would* never turn her back on her new future. Freya was hurting more than Marit could ever imagine for the loss of a future she had wanted with every fibre of her being. And if taking on her duties and role helped Freya in *any* way, Marit would do it. But she would also do it for Aleksander, and for the people of her country, who deserved peace and security and a stable monarchy leading them in uncertain times. She felt that beat as strongly in her heart as her siblings did. She'd just never been called on to prove it. Never been trusted to. So, no. Nothing would stop Marit from returning to Svardia and becoming second in line to the throne.

'I was always going to go back,' she said as he reached for his drink and took a sip. She bit her lip, imagining the burn of alcohol on her tongue, and glanced towards her own drink, waiting for the tremble in her fingers to stop before reaching for it. 'It's just…' The fight to prevent the truth from falling onto the table between them was real.

Just say it. He might hear you.

'There were things I wanted to do. Before I returned to Svardia to take up a royal position that was never meant for me.'

The frown was back, hanging low over his silvery gaze. 'Like what?'

Like, *everything*.

Marit's laugh was heartbreaking to her own ears. 'Like take a walk in the park without a mass of people following my every move.'

'You've never done that?'

'Everyone on the university campus knew who I was. And I was under strict instructions from my parents not to cause trouble.'

'Or what?' Lykos's tone was almost dangerous, his gaze intent, a focus that burned.

She shook her head immediately. 'Nothing like that,' she assured him, understanding the implication in his question. Her parents were never violent, but their disapproval had been almost physical. Descending further in their opinion had always hurt in a way she still couldn't understand. 'But in the end I didn't have time to. I barely scraped a pass for my degree and that took every second of studying there was.' It had been the last promise to her parents, before they'd let her be and do what it was she wanted. Go to university. Get a degree. And then she'd be free.

And less than eight months later everything had changed.

'So, you wanted to go to a blues club without anyone recognising you?' he asked, returning to the original subject of their conversation.

She nodded, blinking back the emotion that threatened to overwhelm her.

'But marriage? To that idiot, André?'

Marit looked at the table. 'It wasn't his finest hour. But he is a good friend. He understood.'

'Understood what?'

'My situation. My future. That my husband will be chosen by the King of Svardia. That he will be titled, as the legislation requires for the second in line to the Svardian throne. That,' she said, a silent sob cutting into her words, 'the first—and last—person I ever kiss will be a stranger.'

Marit hadn't meant to reveal so much. She was usually better at hiding her feelings, or at least plunging them deep beneath an act of rebellion. Why was it this man that called forth the truth from her without even seeming to ask for it?

She reached for her glass, taking a mouthful of the sweet citrus drink, and blamed the alcohol for the sudden rawness in her throat and the jolt to her heart. Lykos turned in his seat and—with the bend of a single finger on a half-raised arm—summoned the waitress. After murmuring something quietly in Italian, she handed over her pad and a pen and disappeared, by which time Marit had swallowed the hitch in her throat and was composed.

'Make a list,' Lykos ordered.

'Of what?' Marit asked, catching the pad and pen he slid across the table.

'Of all the things you want to do before you return to Svardia.'

And, just like that, he surprised her again.

As the early morning's rays pierced through the crack in the curtains, Lykos pinched the bridge of his nose, trying to ward off the migraine that had started shortly after she'd handed him the list she'd made last night.

He should have known better. Really, he should have at least set some parameters. The list had been both shocking and not, and he'd sent her to her suite to order herself room service just to put some space between them. Because last night, instead of seeing Marit as a spoilt runaway princess, or even the key to getting shares in Kozlov's company, he'd seen a young girl being forced into a life she did not want. And it had reminded him of the way his mother used to look at him. Distaste and discomfort had swirled in his gut, leaving him with a bad taste in his mouth even now.

I was always going to go back.

That Marit seemed willing was unfathomable to him, and Lykos wasn't sure that it made anything about the situation remotely okay. He could see what she'd been trying to do with André now. Could even admit that in her position he might have done something similar. He shook his head and cursed.

What was her brother playing at? She was clearly too young to be married off to some stranger and forced to produce heirs like a broodmare. He would never understand that life, their kind. The kind for whom money, tradition and status dictated a life path no one in their right mind would choose. And her future husband would have to be titled. That spoke of extreme snobbery at best, and whispered of eugenics at worst.

But Lykos had made a deal. Unlike his father or

Kyros, when he gave his word he meant it. Even if Marit made him question it. From the moment he'd arrived in London, the sting of Kyros's betrayal burning hot and hard in his heart, Lykos had realised that neither his mentor nor his father were models for the man he wanted to be. So he'd sat in that hotel room and decided: remade himself to who he wanted to be. He would never allow himself to be in that situation again. The only person he could trust was himself. And his words, his acts and his reputation were the only things that could never be taken from him. Aleksander had asked him to keep her from Svardia for five days and he would.

Five days. After her quite spectacular disappearing act, Lykos had imagined he'd spend the entire week trying to catch sand. But since the music venue the fight had gone out of her. The bone-deep defeat had reminded him of his mother and he'd hated seeing the same look in Marit's eyes. So when she'd started talking of things she'd wanted to do before she returned to Svardia, the solution had been clear. He would help her fulfil her wishes, and hopefully that would occupy her enough that she wouldn't cause any more trouble.

Entering the living area, he looked through the French windows to see the sunrise pouring across a pale blue horizon above the Milan skyline as he thought about the list of things Marit had scribbled on the pad. She'd spent such a long time on it that he'd thought her list would fill the entire page. Instead, only seven lines had been filled.

Ice cream in the park.

He'd expected that; after all, she'd said as much in the bar last night.

Eat at a café on the pavement like normal people.

Equally expected and completely doable.

Twenty-four hours out of sight and contact from the world.

Too easy. At this point, Lykos was more than happy to lock her in her room for a day. But some of the others… He squinted at the paper as if it might bring on the headache.

Go to a concert.

A little trickier.

Dance until my feet hurt.

Not impossible.

A tattoo.

His pulse raced a little more. No way was he going to be responsible for returning Marit to Aleksander indelibly marked with ink.

And then there was the last item on the list.

A date.

He felt the vibrations from the slide of the French windows in the adjacent suite and watched Marit walk towards the balcony railing, her hair strands of gold gently rippled by the wind.

He should have left her alone, used the time instead to figure out how on earth he was going to fulfil this list. Maybe even catch up on some sleep, which had been even more elusive than usual. But it was as if there were a piece of string tied between them; where she went he would follow and he felt the tug of it now, low in his gut, undeniable and irrefutable. It was the promise, he told himself as he followed it out onto the balcony.

Marit's gaze stayed locked on the horizon, even though she must have heard the slide of the French windows.

'It's early,' he stated.

'Would you lounge in bed if you had five days of freedom?'

'Yes, actually.'

'Says the man who can do whatever he wants whenever he wants.' She turned to him then, frowning, as if she took in the shadows beneath his eyes. 'You have trouble sleeping.'

He nodded once, surprised that the gesture raised the corner of her lips into a half-smile.

'Your list—'

She raised a hand, cutting him off midsentence. 'I know, they're silly and—'

'We're doing them.' The words cast his promise in stone.

She looked up at him, the sun balancing delicately behind her head, its rays setting her hair on fire, none of which compared to the sparks of golden fire dancing with the slivers of jade in her eyes. She bit her lip as if to prevent just how much it meant to her from escaping, but it failed. He felt her joy, her thanks like a punch to the solar plexus, so powerful he needed a moment to catch his breath.

'But first,' he said, forcing himself not to cast his gaze across her body as he wished, 'clothes.'

She looked momentarily confused, as if she'd forgotten that she'd run from Paris in his shirt and trousers, and then her eyes crinkled with mischief. 'Okay, but Aleksander pays.'

Marit twisted her body in the mirror, surprised by the fit of the wide-legged cropped trousers the shop assistant had promised her would look 'dee-vine'. Marit smiled. She wasn't sure about divine, but the burnt orange heavy cotton did look good. Contrary to the plans she'd had to rack up horrifying bills against her brother's account, she couldn't bring herself to be that wasteful.

Marit might have been overlooked by her parents but she'd always had the greatest of respect for the position their family held and the faith and trust of the Svardian people. Their family's money was the people's money, which was why she'd taken her university degree seriously, even if it hadn't been her choice. Which was the same reason Marit couldn't run up a huge debt just for some clothes.

Something Lykos seemed to be strangely irritated by. She had the sneaking suspicion that it was precisely because he had expected her to, and that made her feel…uncomfortable. Lykos clearly thought she was a spoiled little princess. And while Marit couldn't deny that she had grown up around money—something she instinctively knew Lykos disliked and distrusted—she had never taken that for granted. In the last eight months, her work with the kids in the city youth orchestra had brought her in touch with children from all levels of household income, some of which broke her heart to witness in her country. Just the thought of it made her feel guilty for running off, first with André, then to Milan. To be here now, it just felt…selfish.

With that feeling a dull echo in her heart, she folded up the bare essentials the shop assistant and she had decided on to get her through the next five days, and was about to leave when she heard a tap on the dressing room wall.

'I hope you don't mind, but I was wondering if you might try this on?' said the assistant, a blush on her cheeks at the odd request. 'It's just that my little sister designed the dress. She's working her way through fashion school and I know that it would look incredible on you.' The words rushed out of the proud older sister, and Marit was helpless to refuse.

The moment she was handed the oyster-coloured silk she felt tingles buzz along her skin as if in warning of how precious this moment was. She hung the dress on the hook and, refusing to think too hard on it, slipped out of her clothes and into material that felt like cream against her skin. Gently puffed sleeves gathered at her wrists, framing the V-neck sheath that fitted close to her chest and torso, snugly wrapping around her waist to pour down from her hips to the floor like a waterfall. But it was the hundreds of lines of tiny cream-coloured sequins through the whole dress that made it so magical. They were spaced at different intervals, the closer collection of sequin lines gathering at the front, from where they fell around the V and down, drawing the eye, making Marit look taller and more sophisticated than she'd ever felt.

The lines made her think of music, of sound waves, and although she'd intended to politely refuse the dress, Marit knew that she'd never forgive herself if she didn't take it with her.

The shop assistant gasped when she caught sight of her in the dress—'so beautiful'—the words for the dress as much as Marit, and Marit could only agree.

'Do you want to show your handsome man waiting so patiently out there for you?' she asked.

Something turned in Marit's chest and, biting her lip, she shook her head.

'Ah. Yes, so much better for it to be a surprise,' she whispered conspiratorially.

Marit turned back to look at herself in the mirror without replying, wondering suddenly whether she would ever wear the dress. For some reason she didn't feel that it would be part of her life in Svardia—instinctively knowing that this dress belonged to the five days of freedom a girl called Marit had been given, rather than the Princess who would soon become second in line to the throne. It would be a crime for this dress never to be seen in public and Marit was about to tell the assistant she'd changed her mind, but the woman had already whisked the dress away to be wrapped up.

When she emerged from the dressing room in the small boutique she almost stopped dead in her tracks. Lykos's tall frame lounged in a leather armchair, one leg bent lazily over the other. His elbow was pressed into the arm of the chair, his chin propped up by his thumb and his temple speared by his fingers and, despite the fact that his eyes were closed, he exuded such an air of sensuality that the other customer in the shop had stopped to stare.

Marit's heart stuttered and she pressed her thighs together, trying to quash the pulse of heat that flashed outward across her entire body.

'Are you done?' Lykos asked Marit without opening his eyes.

The other customer squeaked and fled the shop in embarrassment.

'That was cruel,' Marit chided as she went to the counter to make the call to the Svardian embassy to arrange payment.

'She was staring,' he replied, once again with

his eyes closed, making Marit wonder if he had a headache.

'You're handsome. It's not her fault.'

There was a pause before his eyes sprang open and their gazes locked. He looked as if he were about to say something when, thankfully, the embassy answered the phone.

CHAPTER FIVE

His phone buzzed in his trouser pocket but he ignored it, unable to take his eyes off Marit as she charmed the ice cream vendor into providing ice creams for what looked like an entire school bus of children. This was not out of the kindness of the vendor's heart. No. Somehow Lykos was footing the bill.

She turned to look at him directly then, the smile full of bright red lipstick that suited the summery outfit she'd bought from the boutique. Rather than heading straight for stores with famous designers, instead she'd found a little privately owned shop with brightly coloured clothes that reminded Lykos of the films he and Theron used to watch at the open-air screen by the beach in Piraeus.

The dress made Marit's waist look even smaller, cinched by a broad belt, with a skirt that spun out when she turned, the ballet pumps on her feet more comfortable than stylish, but pretty nonetheless. She walked straight to him, perhaps she too was following the invisible thread between them, making his breath catch in his throat in a rather unmanly way, and returned his wallet to the inside pocket of his jacket, the contact shockingly intimate.

'Don't worry, Aleksander will reimburse you.'

Lykos's response of a growl was more grouse than bite, partly because he was trying to control his body's worryingly swift reaction to her touch.

'It is, after all, for the children.' She play-pouted and he rolled his eyes. Spinning away from him, she took up a slow walk down one of the paths in Parco Sempione. Lykos had found it on the internet last night while trying to figure out how to get through Marit's list in the short time that they had. The largest park in Milan boasted lakes and views of the Arch of Peace, as well as being conveniently situated near their hotel.

His eyes scanned the area, the large group of happy children slowly working their way towards a sugar high, teachers trying to wrangle the few stragglers. A couple passed them hand in hand, the dark-haired man making him think of Theron and causing him to wonder how his partner, Summer, was getting on with their new baby. As his attention focused on a young boy, Lykos mentally kicked himself for ignoring Theron's most recent invitation. The baby was cute, he could admit that. But that didn't mean he had to drop everything and rush to admire his friend's progeny. Especially given the baby's biological connection to Kyros Agyros.

He pressed pause on his thoughts and slowed as he saw the young boy move to stand a little too close to the trouser pocket of one of the teachers. And while he might not be overly familiar with children's clothing, he did know clean from dirty, new from old. And he knew a child thief when he saw one. After all, he had been one of the best.

Marit had stopped a few feet ahead and turned to follow the direction of Lykos's gaze. Not wanting to alert the boy, Lykos gave what looked like his full attention to Marit as he pulled his wallet from his pocket discreetly and swapped out his credit card and driver's licence. Marit frowned, clearly realising something was up but thankfully kept her silence. Lykos replaced the wallet in his trouser pocket as he reached Marit and held out his arm to her.

Bemused, Marit took his offer, threading her hand through the crook of his elbow and together they carried on their walk, just like the happy couple they had passed. Lykos wondered how long it would take the boy to notice a much richer mark and, not a minute later, he felt the grab. The boy jolted into him, not too hard, the pressure just right—as if he'd been trying to get round Lykos but misjudged. He imagined the park offered the kid a fair bit of income during the summer months and wouldn't begrudge the loss of the leather wallet at all.

'What was that about?' Marit asked, leaning into his arm conspiratorially after the boy had run off.

'What was what about?' Lykos replied, catching the moment the kid checked the contents of his wallet and saw the boy's eyes grow wide.

'The thing with your cards and your wallet?'

Lykos turned to her, his face purposely blank, but

she wasn't buying it, not for one second. Sighing, he pulled her back onto the path as they made their way towards the Arch. 'Do you see that kid?'

'The one running off?' she asked.

Lykos nodded. 'He just stole my wallet.'

'What?' Marit demanded, shocked. 'Should we call the police?'

Lykos laughed. 'No. He earned it. It was a good lift.' Once again he felt the tug of her confusion. 'If I hadn't expected it, I doubt I would have felt it. It takes years of practice to get that good. And, besides, it was only money. As you saw, I'd removed my cards and ID beforehand.'

'How much was in the wallet?'

Lykos frowned. 'Five, maybe six?'

'Hundred euros?' Marit asked, her voice a squeak.

Lykos shrugged. He had more money than he knew what to do with. What he didn't have—as Kozlov pointed out to anyone who would listen—was pedigree. Unlike Marit. In that moment he knew he had more in common with the kid who'd stolen his wallet than the Princess walking beside him.

'So you let him take a wallet containing six hundred euros?'

'Marit, I know this may be hard for someone like you to understand, but if the kid is stealing wallets he probably needs the money.' Irritation and years old resentment rose to colour his words in harsh tones. And the look of hurt that marred her pretty eyes slapped against his conscience.

She looked at her feet, then off into the distance

where they had last seen the boy. Marit nodded absently and gently withdrew her arm from his, the sudden snap of cold where there had been heat making him feel it even more. He could feel the burn of the blush marking his cheekbones, as much for his guilt as for the shame in what he was about to admit. 'I used to be that kid,' he thrust from between his clenched teeth.

It was her, he realised. It wasn't shame about his humble, if somewhat illegal, upbringing. It was because he didn't want her to look at him like Kozlov. As if he was still that same dirty, streetwise, backtalking kid.

'My father taught me how to steal, how to thieve, as soon as I could walk. By seven years old, he would drop me at a shopping centre and give me a number. If I didn't come back with that amount of money, I'd have to walk home.'

He hadn't spoken to anyone of his past for years. The memories made his throat thicken, his voice gravelly. The muscle at his jaw pulsed and he rolled his shoulders to loosen the tension cording his neck. He felt the furtive touch of her gaze against his cheek, there and gone just as quick, an encouragement to continue.

'My father was a bastard,' he said, simply and truthfully. There had been no redemption for Aeolus Livas. Three years after his mother had left him at the orphanage, Lykos had been caught by some wannabe gangsters Lykos and Theron had tried to rob. One of them, a friend of his father's, recognised

him, let him off the hook for old times' sake with
a drunken mumbled apology for Lykos's loss. That
was how he'd been told about his father's death. As
he'd later found out, he'd crossed the wrong guy and
had been 'dealt with'. And Lykos had never spared
him another thought. Aeolus had been a better drunk
than thief, and a violent husband on a good day. 'But
don't think I didn't use the skills he taught me. I
stole from rich businessmen who wouldn't miss their
money in order to buy food. To buy water.' He shut
his mouth before more revealing words could pour
forth. Thirst. That was what he'd remembered most.
Not the pangs of hunger gnawing at his stomach, or
the fisted grip fear had on his mind, refusing to let
him sleep. Delirious thirst. That had been the worst.

'What about your mother?'

The bright sky fractured into the starburst of a
headache and he winced. 'She did what she had to,'
he replied, coming to the end of the park and hail-
ing a taxi.

'*The only way I'll be safe*,' his mother had said
as she'd left him on the steps of the orphanage, '*is if
he can never use you against me again.*'

Marit was less shocked by the devastating descrip-
tion of his childhood than the way Lykos swayed as
he got out of the taxi at the hotel.

'Lykos—'

'Migraine.'

Pain arced across his features as if even that word
had come at a price. Closing the door to the taxi, she

slid beneath his arm so that she was able to support
him. He looked down at her as if unsettled by her
presence, but his gaze was so unfocused she knew
he was in no position to argue. Benito held open the
door for them and helped Marit up to the suite with
Lykos, sliding the room key over the pad for her as
she took more of Lykos's weight than he would ever
have been comfortable with.

Benito waved off her thanks and retreated back
into the hotel as Marit made her way to the bedroom in a suite that was the mirror image of her
own. She backed them onto the edge of the bed and
when Lykos was safely sitting she went immediately to draw the curtains across the windows, where
the early afternoon's sun stretched rays out towards
them.

There was enough glow from the light of the living room that she could see Lykos's outline but not
so much that it caused him more pain. He tugged at
the buttons on the shirt as he kicked off his shoes,
Marit clenching her jaw seeing the pain even this
seemed to cause him. She'd never had a migraine,
but the headaches she had during her period always
left her shaken. And that was what Lykos looked.
Shaken. His face had lost that natural bronze of his
tan, a slight greyness beneath the sheen of sweat that
looked cold against his forehead. She went to him,
kneeling on the floor, pulling his hand gently back
from where he was struggling with his cufflinks.

'Ridiculous,' he managed.

'It's okay,' she soothed, slipping the cufflink

through the hole and placing it on the floor beside her as if her skin wasn't covered with a thousand pinpricks. She looked up to meet the silvery gaze that found focus on her face and forced herself not to react to the wildfire that burned outwards from her heart to her chest, her legs, her body. His eyes flickered across her as if sensing it, as if tracing the burn patterns he'd caused across her skin, before closing his eyes as if disgusted with himself. For the vulnerability she had seen in him or for the desire he had seen in her, Marit couldn't tell.

Biting back the sting of such obvious rejection, she reached for his other cuff and removed the silver link. As Lykos sat unmoving she inhaled and, making her breath so silent as to not provoke him, she raised onto her knees and reached for the buttons on his shirt. She saw the flare of the muscle at his jaw, as if he was forcing himself still. Or maybe he was simply warding off the migraine. In that moment Marit would have given half of Svardia to know. Because then it would mean she wasn't alone in this crazy thing. The thing that had taken over her pulse and her breathing, that trembled beneath her skin wanting to get out, wanting to bring something in. Wanting *him*.

She slipped the button from its hole, anchoring her bottom lip with her teeth at the sight of the dark swirls of hair, her fingers trembling a little as they moved to free the next button. And the next. She was halfway down his torso when he moved, his chest filling with air and expanding beneath her hands. He leaned side to side, wincing in pain as he lifted the bottom of the shirt from the belted waist of his trousers and exhaled in sufferance. But when his eyes opened, the slice of silver that caught her was molten and fierce. As if she'd woken a slumbering dragon. She paused, caught in an act of theft, having selfishly stolen this moment for herself, only able to breathe when he closed his eyes again. Resisting the urge to shake the tingles that sparked from where her palms had pressed against his body, she slowly slipped the last button from its hole. Swallowing, she turned her face away from the strip of nakedness that tempted her beyond anything she'd ever experienced.

Logically the next step would be his belt and trousers, and the thought burned her cheeks with red slashes. Fingers shaking, she went to reach for his belt and suddenly her hands were caught in a powerful vice. She looked up to find Lykos's eyes clear and full of intent.

'Go.'

She took a breath.

'Now.'

She didn't need to be told twice.

Lykos took stock before he opened his eyes. The pounding in his head was gone and, gently turning from side to side, the severe pain cording his neck with tension had dissipated to almost nothing. He checked the clock and marvelled that he'd slept through the night all the way to seven in the morning.

By now, Lykos knew the drill. Every few months,

the sleeplessness he'd experienced ever since he was a child would catch up with him and he'd have an episode. If he'd been able to return Marit to Svardia she wouldn't have been witness to his weakness. Frustration as much as determination forced him to open his eyes.

Marit. Milan. Cufflinks. *Christé mou*, his belt.

Go. Now.

The look in her eyes as she'd fled the room. The look in her eyes *before* she'd fled the room.

Thank God he hadn't been so out of it last night that he'd reached for all the comfort she was offering, consciously or otherwise. And, just like that, the fantasy of crushing her to him, seeking comfort, an orgasm blowing the migraine from his body... He groaned as need shaped him, hardened him with an arousal that would never be satiated.

He couldn't touch her. She was a princess. She was an *innocent* princess he was charged with protecting. He'd given Aleksander his word and nothing, not even an increasingly urgent desire for her, would stop him from honouring that. Because if he didn't keep his word, all the money in the world wouldn't make him different to his father, or to Kyros. He'd be just like them. Men who betrayed their families, men who betrayed *themselves*. The thought alone was enough to douse the fire in him and force him to the en suite bathroom and beneath the powerful, frigid jets of water in the shower.

He emerged fifteen minutes later, dressed and about to go looking for Marit, when he heard voices out on the balcony. *His* balcony. He took in the strange angle of the pillow and the hotel quilt and realised that Marit must have slept on the sofa. That she'd stayed, even after his harsh order for her to leave... She'd stayed because of her concern for him. That realisation twisted something deep in his gut.

But, *Theé mou*, if he'd known she was within reach...

And, just like that, all the ice-cold shower's good work was undone in seconds. He bit back a curse. Even as a teenager he didn't think he'd been this driven by his hormones. Forcing his body back under control, he made his way out onto the balcony, squinting slightly at the early-morning sun with still-sensitive eyes.

Marit had turned towards the Milan cityscape but Benito greeted him with a small deferential bow, which Lykos immediately waved off.

'I brought Miss Marit some breakfast and coffee. There is fresh fruit, but if you would like something more—'

'*Grazie*, Benito. This is more than fine,' he said, standing by the table. Marit flashed Benito a radiant smile as he left, and returned her gaze to the horizon.

Lykos hovered. Why, he didn't quite know. He wasn't accustomed to hovering, but Marit had this effect on him and he didn't like it one bit.

'About last night—'

'There is nothing to say,' she replied, finally turning to look at him, squinting up into the morning sun.

Lykos opened his mouth.

'Coffee?' she asked. 'I'm sure it's absolutely the worst thing you should do after a migraine, but you don't strike me as a hot water and lemon kind of man.'

It was on his tongue to ask what kind of man she found him, but thankfully he had a few working brain cells left to stop him. Instead, while his grunted response was far from eloquent, it did the job. She poured him a steaming cup of heaven and retreated to her side of the table that she had magicked onto the balcony. Without his notice.

In the last twelve hours, Lykos had shown more vulnerabilities to this one woman than he had to anyone in a lifetime. Bad enough that she'd seen his episode, but that he'd been so out of it that she had slept in the next room and had a table brought through the suite onto the balcony without him stirring?

Unacceptable.

He opened his mouth to speak, but again she cut him off and he barely resisted the urge to growl.

Marit was struggling to meet Lykos's eye. She'd had a terrible night's sleep, which had nothing whatsoever to do with the sofa. No. She'd tossed and turned the entire night because of him. Because of this thing. It was as if a switch had been flipped and now she couldn't stop the…the…things.

Until at around four that morning she'd remembered what had happened before the migraine.

I know this may be hard for someone like you…

It wouldn't take a rocket scientist to pick up on

all the little hints and subtleties at his dislike of her status. The way he said 'Princess', his surprise when she hadn't chosen the most expensive dress or train ticket, or the way he showed more deference to those with lower incomes. It had been strange at first for a billionaire, but what he'd said last night about his father, about growing up on the streets of Athens…

She passed him the cup of coffee she poured him and before she could stop herself she asked, 'How did you get from the streets of Athens to here?'

He stood beside the table looking down at her, holding the small white cup, and the look on his face would have been comical if it hadn't been full of a deep shock that made her wish a thousand times over to take it back. Her question was blunt, untimely and clearly in bad taste. But she hadn't been able to stop herself. She'd spent the entire night tossing and turning, thinking of him as a man and then as a small child, vulnerable to his father's demands…but what about his mother? And how had he ended up on the streets? The uncomfortable silence between them stretched several heartbeats, lasting much longer than she wanted to experience ever again.

'Why, Princess, you'd like to hear my rags-to-riches story?' he mocked. 'You don't believe such a thing can happen?' His questions were bitter and resentful, and utterly justified.

The shame she felt coursing through her from her crass question burned through her, mocking the heat for him she'd felt last night. 'Lykos, I'm sorry. I didn't mean it like that.'

'Then how did you mean it, Princess? Because from where I'm standing—'

'I want to know about you!' The words ripped from her throat, angry and raw. Something changed then. She saw the question reframed in his eyes, the context of last night filtering through to the morning.

'No, Marit. You don't want to know about me.'

Anger, thick and fast, boiled into her bloodstream. How many times had she been told what she did and didn't want? What she could and couldn't do. As if she had no sense of herself, her wants, her desires. Her parents or her siblings, the tutors at university leading her dissertation into an area 'safe' for a princess, safe enough to secure the basic grade she was barely going to scrape.

Her fingers began to itch as her pulse tripped into three-four time. She knew better by now than to fight how people saw her. And she could only imagine how Lykos saw her. Spoiled little princess with no idea of how the world worked. Marit wasn't *that* naïve. She knew there would always be parts of life and the world she would never experience, but that didn't mean she couldn't respect or empathise with those who had different experiences. It had been part of what she'd wanted to achieve with the youth orchestra project. Because one thing she did know was how it felt to not be able to speak of your emotions, feelings that were sometimes bigger than words, that were either impossible to say or would never be heard. But music? It had been a release for her. Through it she'd been able to channel that inexplicable sense of the chaos of her feelings. And she'd wanted so much to help children find that same way of expressing themselves.

Marit nodded, acknowledging Lykos's dismissal, rejection building from a very deep place within her. It was as if someone had whispered *prestissimo* to her body, the blood rushing through her veins as fast as possible. She left without another word, and he let her go.

She passed the sofa she had not slept a wink on, left his suite and swiped her card into hers. She closed the door behind her and resisted the urge to collapse back against it. Instead, she went to the suite's control panel and brought up the sound system settings. She linked her phone to the programme and picked a playlist, turning the volume loud enough to be heard, in all likelihood, above and below. Marit finally didn't care. Because it was also loud enough to drown out the voices that taunted and teased her heart into misery.

Lykos exhaled heavily when the music stopped blaring about three hours later. If he hadn't already recovered from his migraine, the noise from her suite would definitely have brought it on. Any hope he'd had of getting some work done had been obliterated as a classical piece of music swept into a jazzy froth that transitioned into a sassy bluesy number which morphed into a soulful folk song. On the surface, all the pieces were different and had absolutely nothing in common. But Lykos recognised something slith-

ering through each piece, something that spoke of
hurt and hope and need, that pulled at his conscience
for being too harsh on Marit. That same something
that spoke of a complexity he knew Marit had, but
he didn't want to see.

He'd lashed out at her. Yes, her question had
caught him by surprise and, yes, it had been blunt,
but she hadn't deserved his scorn. Yesterday, she
hadn't chosen the most expensive designer labels
to fill her replacement wardrobe with, she'd chosen
a small family-run boutique. She hadn't gorged on
every single ice cream in the park yesterday, she'd
had one and bought the rest for a group of schoolchil-
dren. The list of things she wanted to do before she
returned—it wasn't full of impossibly rich destina-
tions and luxurious experiences—they were things
that she would never get to do once she became second in line to the throne: once she became the female face of Svardian royalty. Once she became a
wife, a mother.

Not that it mattered. She was, and always would
be, a princess.

A princess he was stuck with for another four
days.

His phone pinged again and this time he ignored
it. Thinking back over her question, it was like an
earworm, digging into his thoughts.

I want to know about you!

He felt the difference between Marit's curiosity
and the way that business associates had started to
look at him since Kozlov had unearthed the facts of

his childhood and started spreading rumours. Hers wasn't the eager glee, poring over his poverty, abuse and betrayals as if they were a form of entertainment. But what Lykos couldn't account for was the urge to tell her about it.

Before he could change his mind, he left the suite and knocked on the door to Marit's. He spent so long imagining her response when she opened the door that it took him a moment to realise that she *wasn't* there.

Anger flashed through his entire body. The music, the volume—a ruse? She had run away again and he had fallen for it entirely. Her sweetness and innocence—it was all an act. Cursing, he returned to his suite, thankful that this time he could find his wallet and phone, and, refusing to wait for the lift, took the fire escape stairs all the way down to the ground floor, unwilling to lose another precious second.

CHAPTER SIX

LYKOS BURST FROM the door at the side of the hotel onto the pavement, startling a dog walker and causing the little beast to howl disapprovingly. Inside, he felt...betrayal, the cold, hard, familiar twist of it turning in his gut. And stupid. He felt stupid. He was usually much more careful than this, better at seeing through people's lies. He'd had to be. But he'd been distracted by a pretty face and a princess's tantrum.

No. He'd been distracted because he thought he'd seen the truth in her eyes when she'd claimed to want to know about him. A *princess*. And now she'd run. He should have known better. His heart was pounding heavily in his chest, not from the run but from *her*.

He cursed loudly in Greek and fisted his hand. It caught Benito's attention and he came rushing over.

'Signor—'

'Have you seen her?' he asked, his gaze sweeping back and forth across the street.

'Miss Marit? Yes, she asked about a street café and I directed her to Carlotta's.'

'What?' Lykos asked, his brain trying to clear through the damp fog of his thoughts, unable to understand why Marit would have asked Benito about a café. Unless it was another misdirect, his cynical mind suggested.

'Carlotta's. It's by the park. I'll send you the directions I gave Miss Marit.'

Lykos started jogging in the direction Benito had gestured and, pulling his phone from his pocket when it pinged, he realised he had several missed calls and text messages. He frowned. No one texted him these days. He pulled down the top bar and saw that just beneath a work email were four text messages from a number he'd programmed into his phone two days ago.

Didn't want to bother you, but got a little hungry and thought I'd cross something off my list. Benito knows where I am if you want to join me, but no pressure.

PS This is Marit. I'm assuming you have my number.

PPS And clearly you could track my phone should you wish.

His jog slowed to a walk as he read Marit's first message, and he slowed to a stop as he read the next and the next. Each one threw his feelings into even more confusion until he felt vaguely nauseous. She hadn't run from him this time.

He looked up and saw tables and chairs spilling onto the open square beneath an awning that said 'Carlotta's' in bright blue against brilliant white. At one of the tables he saw her, a cascade of beautiful golden hair and a pair of hazel eyes staring at him. Eyes that morphed from pleased to hurt, before the shutters came down as a waiter brought her a bulbous glass of something bright orange. Her smile to the café's employee was glorious and generous and the poor boy looked as if he'd been struck by lightning. Lykos walked towards Marit's table, unable to take his eyes from her, sliding his phone in his pocket before taking the seat opposite her.

'You thought I'd run,' she accused, glancing towards him, unable to hide the hurt that marred her features.

His stomach twisted, but he wouldn't do her the dishonour of lying to her. 'Yes.'

She turned her head aside in the most gracious of cuts and a conscience he seemed to have grown only in the last two days jabbed and prodded again. He called the waiter over with a raise of his finger, his gaze still locked on Marit. He ordered a beer, not his usual drink but it was early in the day and for some reason he felt a nostalgic pull towards it.

'I don't think I've had a beer since I was with Theron in Piraeus over ten years ago,' he revealed. Nothing in him ever wanted to discuss his past. But with Marit? It was especially hard with her. It felt as if it would create an even greater divide between the Princess and the one-time pauper. But she had asked because she wanted to know and, instinctively, he felt it would be a peace offering that she'd understand. And maybe if they stopped fighting each other and kept that truce he would stop feeling this twisting frustration that had him by the gut. Maybe if he answered her question from that morning the desire he saw burning golden flecks in her hazel eyes would burn to dust.

'I met Theron about two years after my mother left me at the orphanage. I was nine and he was seven. His parents had been killed in an earthquake that devastated Athens and he was so wide-eyed and scared.' Lykos shook his head thinking about the vulnerable little boy his oldest friend had been back then. 'Of course he'd kill me for telling you that,' he said, allowing the bond of friendship to pull his lips into a small smile. A friendship they'd only just rekindled. He paused while the waiter placed the beer in front of him and stared at it a beat before reaching for the condensation-covered glass.

'We were the scourge of Athens,' he announced with pride, tipping his drink upward in a toast, a title thoroughly earned and utterly justified. 'No businessman's wallet was safe, no unsuspecting tourist's camera and phone protected. One time, we stole a whole tray of muffins from a coffee vendor. Theron tells me the old man has neither forgotten nor forgiven it,' he said with the huff of a laugh.

Marit's gaze was drawn by his words, her eyes sparkling as he told her more stories of the easy, gentle thievery he and Theron had used to get up to.

No one ever left out of pocket too badly and no one ever hurt. He told her about lifting Kyros Agyros's wallet. How Theron's soft heart had made him insist they returned it to the billionaire businessman when he'd seen a picture of the man dancing with his wife.

'Kyros was...' Lykos shook his head, feeling that powerful force he'd first felt when he'd met the older man '...impressive. Rich. *Very* rich,' he said wryly. 'What he saw in two street kids, I'll never know. But he made us an offer. He paid for our education, trained us, taught us everything we could learn, with the condition that we went to work for him after finishing school and national service. And every Sunday he invited us for dinner at his house with his wife, Althaia.' His heart twisted with grief from her passing three years ago, despite not having seen her for over ten years.

Marit frowned, as if noticing the swift turn in his feelings. 'I'd never been foolish enough to look up to Kyros the way that Theron did—' *Liar*, his newly vocal conscience claimed. 'But I did respect him. Until he sent me looking for an Englishwoman. An Englishwoman with a little girl who had Kyros's eyes.'

And, just like that, the scales had fallen from his eyes. His mentor wasn't the kind, devoted married businessman, determined to help two kids from the streets, to treat them like the sons he'd never had. No, Kyros Agyros was just like everyone else: ready to use Lykos's debt to buy his silence.

'Oh.' There was a glimmer of understanding in

Marit's eyes and he could see the pulse flicker at her throat, her soft heart beating with too much empathy.

'Kyros's wife was ill. She had multiple sclerosis. For Althaia it was a life sentence, and it made Kyros's betrayal so much worse.' Anger coloured his words with gravel and sand. 'I presume he sent me thinking I would be so grateful that I'd not say anything to Althaia.' Kyros's betrayal had cost Lykos everything: the family unit he'd never thought he'd have after his mother's abandonment disappearing in the blink of an eye.

'Instead of going back to Greece, I went straight to a small hotel in London.' It had been years since Lykos had allowed himself to think of those first few days. The blinding pain of being used and betrayed by the man he'd thought of as his *true* father. The shocking blow to his sense of self and everything he'd known had brought on a migraine so bad Lykos had almost called an ambulance. But when the aura of agony had receded, Lykos felt a clarity of thought he'd not experienced before.

'While I was there, I used the money I'd saved from the two years working for Kyros to play the stock markets.' For the first time, Lykos's sleeplessness had become a benefit. During the late-night hours he'd hunted the stock markets for quick hits and even quicker sales, surprised to find that the lessons he'd learned from his father—misdirection, disguise, speed and intense focus—had become a transferable skill. Kyros's act of betrayal had further forced a complete trust in himself and his own instincts.

But those skills were the only thing from his past that Lykos chose to take with him into the future. From that moment on, he promised he'd never trust anyone but himself. He'd chosen the tenets he would live by: his words, his acts and his reputation. His future was severed irrevocably from his past as a thief from the streets of Athens.

'Within a month I had doubled my savings,' he said, no trace of arrogance tainting the statement of fact, no hint of the negative bent of his thoughts. 'Within the first year my name was a whispered warning, and in five years I had majority shares in more companies than I could remember the names of.'

Over the years, more and more companies had required face-to-face meetings and, after his childhood on the streets, he had settled easily into a nomadic way of life in luxury hotels across Singapore, Zurich, New York, Hong Kong, Toronto, Sydney and here in Milan. Not once in all that time had anyone peered too closely at his past. Not once in all that time had anyone *wanted* to know.

Until Kozlov.

Until *Marit*.

'And that is how I got from the streets of Athens to here,' he said, finally taking a sip of his beer, the amber liquid tasting like memories and regret.

Marit didn't think Lykos had meant to reveal so much, but she'd been able to see through his words to the betrayal he had felt at the hands of his mentor. After a father who had given Lykos nothing but abuse and mistreatment, to be used by a man he'd thought was safety and hope personified…it must have been devastating for him. Yet he simply shrugged dismissively as if it hadn't cost him a thing.

'It's an incredible achievement,' she said sincerely.

He simply inclined his head as if acknowledging the truth of her observation while not taking the praise. Marit reached for her drink. The large slice of orange soaking in the midday sun made the drink look frivolous, not to mention the candy-striped straw and the little cocktail umbrella.

Lykos swallowed, put his beer back onto the thick white cotton covered table, leaned forward and nudged the paper umbrella before she could pick up the glass. 'You and your sweet tooth.' He tutted as if disappointed, the tease pulling at the corner of her mouth, anchoring her in the present and away from the shadowy images he had painted in her mind of a childhood that couldn't have been more different from her own.

He leaned back in his chair, his gaze holding her enthralled, forgetting her drink, forgetting their fight and once again that awareness twisted and turned deep within her. It smashed the defences she'd built last night and suddenly they were back in that darkened room, her breath caught in her lungs, his chest beneath her palms—

'What was growing up like for a princess?'

His question snapped her back into the present as

if she were on a leash he held and because she was so distracted the truth fell from her lips.

'Lonely.'

They both blinked at her answer and she shook her head, trying to understand why this man seemed the only person to whom she said what she never wanted to say. Focusing on picking at an imaginary bit of fluff from her trouser leg, she had marshalled her features by the time she looked back up at him, her voice cool as she said, 'I'm sure you don't want to hear about the poor little Princess.'

He held her gaze and in it she heard her words to him earlier that day. *I want to know about you!*

She would have given anything to hear him say that. It made her cheeks pink and her heart turn. He was stubborn enough to keep on staring at her in silence until she answered his question, even if it took all afternoon.

'There are little girls all around the world who dream of being a princess,' she said.

'Not you?'

Marit shook her head and shrugged easily. 'How can you dream of what you already are?'

Only she wasn't. Not really. Freya was the real Princess. Loved by the people and her parents and, despite the sting of jealousy, loved by Marit most of all. The absence of her parents' attention—love—had always made her feel *invisible*. As if she didn't matter. As if her thoughts and feelings weren't important. But it had been Freya who came to her room when Marit had a nightmare. Freya who soothed her tears when she fell over. Freya who told Aleksander to stop being a beast for hiding her toys. Freya who helped get Marit out of the palace maze when one of their nannies got distracted. But even Freya hadn't quite been able to compensate for the lack of love Marit received from their parents.

'So, you are what you always wanted to be?' he asked, the doubt in his tone making it clear he too thought little of her being a princess.

'I wanted to be a musician,' she said, wanting to pierce the arrogance of his response. 'But a royal cannot be such a thing.'

'Who decided that?'

Marit stifled the urge to make a pithy comment, to hide her hurt in a joke or a distraction, but Lykos had honoured her with the truth and she would not disrespect him in return. 'My parents. It wasn't up for debate,' she said, taking a sip of her Aperol Spritz, not tasting the sweet orange and herby bitterness of it at all.

'What were they like?' His silvery gaze glinted in the afternoon sun and she couldn't shake the sense that he was hunting her response for something that would explain who she was on a level she didn't want him to see.

'They were the King and Queen of Svardia.'

He levelled her with that gaze that demanded answers, demanded honesty.

'They were distracted and very busy. Always in meetings, or on trips to far-flung countries,' she said simply. 'Papa wasn't supposed to have ruled, but his brother died in an accident before he had heirs, so he was propelled into a position I don't think he wanted.' It was the first time she had said the words out loud and the first time she wondered for the space of a heartbeat if she might have something in common with the stern-jawed, dark-eyed man who was her father. That he had never been meant to rule had always made Marit wonder if that was somehow to blame for the way her parents immersed themselves so deeply into the role that they rarely looked up. 'But he certainly made sure that Aleksander and Freya knew their roles and their future responsibilities.'

'And you?'

'The only expectation for me was to stay out of trouble.' So simple, and yet so damaging too. At dinners, their parents tested and prepared her siblings. Even if Freya tried to bring her into the conversation, it never lasted long. Aleksander had watched with a kind of helpless fury which had only made things worse and, in the end, Marit had settled with trying to make the silent waiting staff react to little silly pranks unseen by her parents.

'Well, that worked out well.'

She held her hands up in mock surrender. 'It was absolutely not my fault that the son of the German ambassador ended up with cherry juice all down his front just seconds before the photographs.'

Lykos raised an eyebrow.

'He got handsy! And how on earth was I supposed to know that my skirt was tucked into my knickers on the red carpet on the New Year's Eve parade?'

Lykos choked on his beer. 'What about the suspension from boarding school?' he demanded when he'd recovered.

'Yes, okay. I'll admit to that, but—'

'And the skiing trip that cut your mother's trip short when you were fourteen?'

It was as if a knife sliced through the afternoon, silently knocking the air from her lungs. Marit hated that this one moment in her history still had such a debilitating effect on her. She tried to smile it off, but Lykos had seen, she could tell by the way he leant forward across the table, the way his eyes narrowed.

'What?'

'What?' she asked in response, as if she had any hope of covering it.

'Marit.' His voice was a warning.

'Ah, yes. The infamous skiing trip that ruined my parents' very important trip to Japan,' she said, her tone full of a humour that hurt. 'The one where my mother was photographed leaving the private plane chartered to return her home. Snapped on the steps of the hospital looking so very concerned as she spoke to the senior surgeon. And even caught in the act of shaking the hands of the nurses that had helped care for her daughter. The one,' Marit said, unable to conceal the years' old hurt from her voice, 'where my mother never actually came to see me. *That* skiing trip.'

Marit hated that she sounded like such a child. Hated that it made her want to cry. In front of this man who had endured so much worse. Did he know just how embarrassing it was to admit that her mother couldn't even be bothered to come and see her in the hospital? That Marit mattered so little to her.

She wished she could make him understand. But how could she explain the agony of the loneliness of her childhood? The anguish of feeling invisible in a palace full of people. As if she were screaming and no one heard her.

Lykos ground his teeth together to prevent the words from coming out of his mouth. Was he guilty of seeing her cynically, as 'the poor little Princess'? Absolutely. Could he understand why her parents couldn't conceive of her as a musician? Probably. He wasn't sure why it seemed unfathomable, but it did. But for her mother to cancel a trip, ensure that she was photographed arriving at her child's sickbed and not visit the child?

Lykos had been forced to grow up quickly and, although he'd never admit it to a living soul, he'd still never stopped wanting his mother. There was only one reason he had stayed away from her all this time and that was because it had been her request. But Marit's mother had been at the hospital and *not* seen her child. He just couldn't comprehend it.

'Were you unconscious when she visited?'

Marit looked up, blonde hair gently curling in the wind, eyes wide as if half afraid that closing them would release the tears he could see gathering. She risked it and only one fell, but Marit didn't seem to notice it as it slipped down her cheek. The sight of it tore at something deep in his chest.

'No. She left before I was out of surgery.' She shook her head and painted on a smile. 'Freya arrived so it was okay.'

'When did she arrive?'

'As soon as she could.'

'When?'

'Three hours after I'd woken up.'

Finally, as if she were too tired to fight any more, the mask dropped and he saw it. The hurt, the rejection—so different to his own yet so familiar. How had it taken him this long to recognise it in her? Was that why he reacted so strongly to her? He was normally infallible when it came to seeing what people wanted to hide; when had he become arrogant in his assumption that she was simply the spoiled runaway Princess?

Christé mou, he cursed. There was nothing spoiled about her.

The waiter came to enquire about their drinks and, checking his watch, Lykos asked Marit if she was ready to tick something off her list. The smile on her face and the brightness in her eyes was his reward and someone dropped a glass and Lykos didn't even notice.

They ordered lunch and Lykos moved the conversation to easier things, partly so he could take in and reframe all that he knew about her. She ordered a pizza and ate it with her hands, laughing more in the sunshine than he could have imagined. He had pasta, but he'd never be able to say what sort it was because the only thing he remembered of that afternoon was feeling lighter than he had done since he could remember.

While she was freshening up his phone rang and, absentmindedly, he answered.

'What are you up to, Livas?' The Russian accent coming through the phone's earpiece was thick and harsh in the Italian sunshine.

'Actually, I've decided to take a bit of a holiday.'

'You don't do holidays. But to find that you *do* blondes is interesting to me. Princess Marit, she's quite a beauty. Though what she's doing with a street thug like you, I've no idea.'

No one watching Lykos would think that he felt anything in response to the Russian's statement. But deep down he was as close to violence as he had ever been. His pulse rocketed from nought to sixty and he felt a cold sweat break out across his shoulders. 'She has nothing to do with you, Kozlov.'

'On the contrary, she is the sister of the man who owns a number of shares in my company and is therefore of *great* interest to me.'

'It's a rather large number of shares, from what I hear,' Lykos warned, reacting immediately to the implied threat to Marit.

His accent harsh and anger dripping from each word, Kozlov's response was a guttural growl. 'I've allowed you to chase the scraps I have cast aside because it amused me. But no more.'

The line went dead just as Marit appeared from the back of the restaurant.

Kozlov's threat circled in Lykos's mind and fury burned incandescent within him. Swallowing the fiery heat of his rage, he marshalled his features with a ruthlessness honed over many years. While Marit was walking though the restaurant, completely unaware of the waiter's puppy-dog eyes, Lykos's mind processed options at the speed of light.

That Kozlov knew about Marit now was untenable, and the first chance he got he would call Aleksander to warn him. Kozlov might see the shareholder as a threat now that the Svardians had been linked to him, Lykos realised. A cold, hard fist gripped him. He would never put Marit in danger.

In the space of a heartbeat, Lykos was six years old, skinny, thin and utterly helpless against the sound of violence in the room next door. A tremor rose within him, cracking and fracturing the stone seal he'd placed on the memories of those nights. *The only way I'll be safe is if he can never use you against me again.* A cold sweat broke out across the back of his neck and as Marit approached, bringing sunshine and warmth with her back to the table, he still felt as if he had plunged his hands into an oil slick.

No. This time he would get it right. He would protect her.

She sat down and was about to say something, but she frowned, choosing something entirely different to ask instead. 'What's wrong?'

'We have to go.' The words ground out of him as he signalled to the waiter.

'Back to the hotel?'

'Yes. But only to pick up our things.'

'Why?' she asked, confusion clouding the precious shards he loved seeing in her eyes.

'We're going to London.'

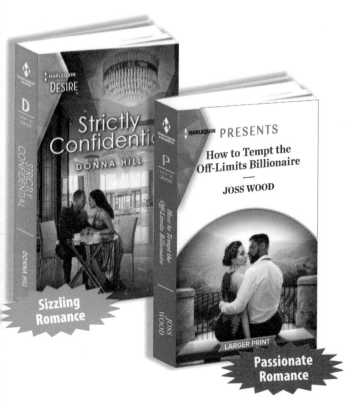

**Claim up to FOUR NEW BOOKS & TWO MYSTERY GIFTS –
absolutely FREE!**

Dear Reader,

We both know life can be difficult at times. That's why it's important to treat yourself so you can relax and recharge once in a while.

And I'd like to help you do this by sending you this amazing offer of up to FOUR brand new full length FREE BOOKS that WE pay for.

This is everything I have ready to send to you right now:

Try **Harlequin® Desire** books featuring the worlds of the American elite with juicy plot twists, delicious sensuality and intriguing scandal.

Try **Harlequin Presents® Larger-Print** books featuring the glamorous lives of royals and billionaires in a world of exotic locations, where passion knows no bounds.

Or TRY BOTH!

All we ask in return is that you answer 4 simple questions on the attached Treat Yourself survey. You'll get **Two Free Books** and **Two Mystery Gifts** from each series you try, *altogether worth over $20*! Who could pass up a deal like that?

Sincerely,

Pam Powers

Harlequin Reader Service

Treat Yourself to Free Books and Free Gifts.

Answer 4 fun questions and get rewarded.

◄ DETACH AND MAIL CARD TODAY!

	YES	NO
1. I LOVE reading a good book.	○	○
2. I indulge and "treat" myself often.	○	○
3. I love getting FREE things.	○	○
4. Reading is one of my favorite activities.	○	○

TREAT YOURSELF • Pick your 2 Free Books...

Yes! Please send me my Free Books from each series I select and Free Mystery Gifts. I understand that I am under no obligation to buy anything, as explained on the back of this card.

Which do you prefer?
- ❏ **Harlequin Desire®** 225/326 HDL GRAN
- ❏ **Harlequin Presents® Larger-Print** 176/376 HDL GRAN
- ❏ **Try Both** 225/326 & 176/376 HDL GRAY

FIRST NAME   LAST NAME

ADDRESS

APT.#   CITY

STATE/PROV.   ZIP/POSTAL CODE

EMAIL ❏ Please check this box if you would like to receive newsletters and promotional emails from Harlequin Enterprises ULC and its affiliates. You can unsubscribe anytime.

© 2022 HARLEQUIN ENTERPRISES ULC
® and ® are trademarks owned by Harlequin Enterprises ULC. Printed in the U.S.A.

HD/HP-520-TY22

CHAPTER SEVEN

MARIT GAZED OUT of the window of the car winding its way from a private airfield on the outskirts of London through city streets bathed in a teal-coloured dusk. She refused to look at the self-made Greek billionaire who had remained thin-lipped and grim with determination throughout their journey. Something had happened while she'd been freshening up in the bathroom and by the time she'd returned to the table the warm glow of an afternoon spent with someone she had come to admire, to find amusing, both of which had been more of a shock than the almost constant pull of awareness she felt to him, was gone. She thought they'd made a connection, shared an understanding that had made her feel…seen.

She almost laughed at herself for being so foolish. Before Lykos had come along, she'd made her peace with stepping into her sister's shoes. She'd even begun to hope that finally she might be able to prove herself worthy of her title, finally able to exceed the expectations her family had always lowered for her. In some way, André had been part of that peace. It wasn't love. They hadn't even kissed. But they'd both hoped their friendship would be enough to get them through their futures.

And then Lykos had barged into her hotel room and everything had changed.

Sharing ice cream in the park, having lunch together, sharing confidences… She had felt like a sunflower turning towards the sun, she had felt her soul sparkle when he'd teased her, when he'd been impressed by her. She'd found herself wanting to earn his admiration, his respect, his *affection*. It had shown her what had been and what would be missing from her life after she returned to Svardia. It had made her want to reach out to him, hold him to her for the short while they had.

Until he had whisked them from Milan to London. His withdrawal from her, the meaningful silence between them, felt horribly similar to how her parents had often been with her. But somehow this hurt more. She shivered at the thought and, without word or question, Lykos simply adjusted the temperature controls. With her gaze on the crowds of people flocking the central London streets, even at this time of the early evening, she unclenched her jaw. 'Why are we in London?'

Turning in the silence between them, she found his gaze locked on her. And because she was looking so intently herself, she saw it. The moment the lie formed in his mind.

'We're here for your date.'

She swallowed the wave of hurt that threatened

to clog her throat with tears. 'My date?' she asked, her lips strangely numb.

'Yes. On your list. We're going on your date tonight.'

'How lovely,' she replied, while inside something curled in on itself, irrevocably wounded. For just a moment back in Milan, Marit had trusted him, found comfort with him, happiness even, and Lykos had lied to her, obliterating any sense of connection she'd felt.

She'd had it all wrong, she realised. He'd never seen her at all.

Lykos had called Aleksander while Marit had slept on the private jet. The King had offered the support of the security services, but Lykos had refused. More people meant more attention and more notice. Years ago, he'd learned that small meant quick, nimble and often invisible. As such, keeping it to him and Marit was actually the safer option. Aleksander had agreed, but his embassy was on alert and he gave Lykos a direct telephone number that would be changed the moment Marit was back on Svardian soil.

Lykos appreciated the reminder and it became a mental line in the sand. After he returned Marit to Svardia, everything would go back to normal. He'd have the shares to bring Kozlov down and be able to return to the nomadic lifestyle that he enjoyed: hotels in every city, a willing woman in every bar who'd appreciate a brief encounter as much as he did. No one to ask meaningful questions, no one to dig deeper than he wished. His future was as he liked it, on his terms and his terms only: alone and uncomplicated.

He looked out of the window, wondering why it felt a little hollow.

We're here for your date.

It had been the only reason he could think of to explain why they had left Milan and now Lykos was taking Marit on a date. Which was very complicated. He clenched his jaw as he called himself every single kind of fool. He could tell that Marit was upset by his withdrawal, but his intention to break the connection forming between them had been for her own good. And then he'd gone and told her he was taking her on a date.

The car pulled up outside the black iron railings that fronted the Regency terrace townhouse he'd bought after a year in London. He had wanted it on first sight. It was everything that he'd not been, everything that he'd not had growing up: money, history, permanence, sophistication. It wasn't quite a castle, but it wasn't far off.

Beside him, Marit was staring up at the townhouse with a frown.

'This is yours?'

'Yes,' he said, pride and satisfaction infusing his tone. 'You don't like it?'

'I do,' she said, peering through the car window, still taking in the perfect façade. 'It just doesn't feel like you.' With that she exited the car, closing the door behind her and leaving him feeling…confused.

He got out. 'What do you mean?' he called over

the roof of the car, but she was through the gate and had followed the driver with their luggage to the front door.

Unlike his properties in Europe, this purchase had nothing to do with convenience. He'd had a large amount of work done restoring or recreating as much of the original fixtures and mouldings as possible because, while it was everything his childhood hadn't been, it was exactly what he wanted in his future. It was why he'd teased Theron with his desire to buy the Soames estate, which was as close to a castle as one could get. Lykos had always wanted that grandeur, something that would *endure*, a level of class that would protect him from the harm done to him in the past. At least that was how it had felt to him until Marit had taken one look and seen right through it.

When he reached her at the front door she turned to him, the security light turning her hair even more golden and her eyes glistening. 'It is perfect for the financial genius that stalks international stock exchanges,' she assured him.

He opened the door with the press of his thumb to the security pad, realising that her final observation didn't make him feel much better, and ushered her through to the hallway. He picked up their luggage and brought it across the threshold to find her standing there, hands held to her chest, something else clearly on her mind.

He put down their bags as her lips quivered into a reluctant smile. 'I've never been on a date before.'

Theé mou, she was too innocent even to be in his

company. That he was taking her on her first date…
she deserved so much better. She deserved—

'I'm glad it's you,' she said, looking up at him,
the truth of her words shining in her eyes. 'Don't
get me wrong,' she rushed to say. 'I know that this
is because of my list, that this isn't real. Not really,'
she said with a shrug of her shoulder that made him
want to argue with her, to disagree wholeheartedly.
'But it's not and I think it would have been worse if
it had been.'

'Why?' Curiosity meant the question sprang from
his lips before he could call it back.

'Because…' She frowned, little lines marring her
forehead as she sought the right words. 'Because if
I had to return to Svardia and marry a man of my
brother's choosing after feeling…more for someone
else, I think that would have been a tragedy.'

It was as if she'd struck him with a knife and
twisted, all the while smiling prettily as if nothing were horrifying about what she'd just said. She
hadn't meant 'more', she'd meant love. And in that
one sentence, Lykos realised what it *really* meant for
her to return to Svardia and marry a man appropriate for the second in line to the throne.

An hour later Marit stood before the mirror in the
guest room and turned, watching the way the sequins
flashed and flickered in beautiful lines running
down the front of the dress like streams of water.
As the only dress she had with her, there hadn't even
been a choice, for which she was thankful as she

might not have had the courage to wear it otherwise. Against the oyster-coloured silk, the cream sequins were only visible when they caught the light and were more breathtaking for it.

Marit looked at a reflection that she had never seen before. The dress clung to curves that were womanly, elegant and beautiful. She didn't feel like a child playing dress-up. She felt…like *her*. Like how she was supposed to be seen. The silk fell from low on her hips and rippled into fluted waves that looked nothing short of luxurious and the deep V at her breast was short of indecent but long past conservative.

She leaned into the mirror to put the last sweep of mascara to her eyelashes, and if she had to blink a little to press back the desire for this entire evening to be real then that was what she had to do. The little antique bronze clock on the table beside the large bed clicked over to seven, chiming prettily seven times, announcing the hour Lykos had told her the car would arrive to take them on their date.

But in her heart it rang for something else. This was her third night and she was just over halfway through the time she had left. Pressing a hand to her sternum to soothe her heart, she realised that it wasn't the return to Svardia that was feeding the sense of urgency in her breast. Actually, she was beginning to hope that she could show her parents, her siblings that she could do it, that she *could* be trusted in Freya's role.

But she was painfully aware of the experiences

she would miss when she did. And her list—the seemingly simple experiences she'd given to Lykos to complete—to have those without the judgemental eyes of the press or public on her...they would have to be enough to leave her with memories in a future of confinement. Like tonight. A last freedom. With that determination steeling her backbone, she left the room ready to face whatever the evening held.

The town car pulled up outside what looked to Marit like another row of stunning English townhouses. Residential, she thought, wondering if they were to visit a friend of Lykos, which felt a little peculiar for a date, but who was she to know? Then she noticed two men in dark suits standing, as if to attention, either side of a door with such slick black gloss it looked as if it had been raining.

She looked across the dark interior of the town car to where Lykos was once again watching her, the hairs on the back of her neck riffled by the feel of his eyes on her.

'You look incredible,' he said again. He'd said it the first time she'd come down the stairs to find him waiting for her. She hadn't wanted to hear it, didn't want his false flattery, but there had been a tone in his voice, a subtle bass chord beneath an arcing tremble of treble notes, and she'd felt it. She'd wanted to believe him then, just as she did now. And, just like before, she nodded, before looking back to the strange place they'd come to.

Lykos exited the car and stood on the pavement as

the driver opened her door. Placing one hand in the driver's and picking up her skirts in the other, she stepped out of the car and onto the pavement. She tried to ignore him, but her skin was scorched by Lykos's gaze and she felt it everywhere. The driver presented her to Lykos like a prize, something to be cherished, and when Lykos held his arm out for her to take she wondered if it would be so bad to just pretend. Just for tonight. That he was a devastatingly handsome man unable to keep his eyes from her because he wanted her just as much as she wanted him. She so desperately wanted him to want her, not because she was needed, not because she was a means to an end, like the shares, or the role she was about to step into, but for who she was.

Her breath caught in her lungs and came out in a sigh the moment she gave in to the fantasy and went to stand, arm tucked in his, beside him. He looked down at her, his face half hidden in the shadows of the fast-approaching night. 'Nervous?' he asked, concern rather than his usual tease striking a discordant note.

'Not with you,' she answered honestly, and the shadows cleared in his gaze for just a heartbeat before he turned to face their destination, pulling once at each cufflink before leading them to the door.

'Mr Livas,' said one of the men, a small but deferential bow accompanying his words, while the other man pushed open the door. 'Welcome to Victoriana, Princess Marit.'

Marit looked back over her shoulder at the man

who had welcomed her by name. 'Did you call ahead?' she asked Lykos in a whisper.

He shook his head. 'The staff here are as well informed as they are discreet,' he explained as they were greeted by a woman wearing what looked like a costume from the English Victorian period. The hostess wore a waistcoat over a white shirt with some kind of old-fashioned cropped trousers, looking oddly stylish. Marit and Lykos were led down a dark hallway with wooden panels and a tartan carpet in dark browns and creams that made her feel cocooned until the hallway opened out into an inconceivably large room. Literally inconceivable as it was bigger on the inside than on the outside.

Unable to help herself, Marit spun in a circle, trying to take in her surroundings. A long bar made of green swirling marble ran the length of what she realised must have been at least two houses brought together. Behind it stood men and women also dressed in the same Victorian clothing, mixing brightly coloured cocktails. There were wooden plaques above doorways leading off the central area with gold cursive announcing 'The Library', 'The Billiard Room', 'The Orangery', as if the place was some old English country house.

Lykos, beside her, gestured for Marit to follow the hostess, who wove her way through tables that had discreet, gentle lighting to a doorway where Marit's feet faltered when she read the plaque above it. 'The Music Room'. Lykos drew to a stop behind her, the heat of his body blanketing her. Her heart pulsed with useless longing that she knew Lykos would never entertain and shook off the moment to follow the hostess into a room that took Marit's breath away.

A chandelier hung into the centre of a large room, with a fireplace that might have dominated the room entirely had it not been for the grand piano that stole all of her attention. She had vague impressions of dark panelled wood, bookcases and pampas grass. Dark greens, burgundies and gold, but it was the perfect sound of the clearly very well cared for musical instrument that sounded like silken threads filling the air in the room. Threads that wound into her heart and pulled it into the sky.

The pianist seemed lost in his music and for just a moment Marit enjoyed the image of it, the fantasy of the Victorian music room. She turned to Lykos, knowing that he'd done this, that he'd tried to shape this evening around her and what she liked, and it meant so much more than he'd ever know. He might have withdrawn from her reach, but he had given her what he could. He had given her *this*.

He looked at her, his eyes skimming over her features as if he were mentally recording her reaction and, once satisfied, gestured for her to take a seat. There were a few other tables in the room, couples seated close together, gently whispered words that couldn't be heard but made a beautiful backdrop. Their presence made Marit feel more discreet as they become anonymous in the company of the room.

Marit took a seat at the small table where she could see the piano player best and tried to ignore the way she felt when Lykos sat, not opposite her but at an angle next to her. A drink was placed to her left and a different drink was placed beside Lykos by a waiter so discreet Marit barely saw him leave.

She stared at the tumbler, a white froth above a rich amber, topped with a twirl of orange peel and a bright glossy cherry.

'What is it?' she asked, looking up at Lykos.

'You'll love it,' he said with a confidence that sang to the blood rushing in her veins.

She reached for her drink when his voice stopped her.

'Marit…' He paused. Shook his head a little, clenching his jaw so that she could see the flex of muscle there. He took a deep breath. 'Marit, if you don't want to go back—'

'To Svardia?' she asked in shock.

'I will not make you. So if you want—'

Her fingers pressed against her lips to stop the tumble of words on the tip of her tongue because, for just a second, she feared she wasn't strong enough to refuse his offer. Her shock had stopped his words, the concern in his eyes so much, too much for Marit to bear. He reached for her but she shook her head, and his hand stopped inches from her elbow.

If he failed to return her to Svardia, there was no way her brother would give Lykos the shares he needed. He would give that up for her? She couldn't think about what that meant for her, for him. It was too much. As her heart began to settle and she forced herself to think through her feelings she smiled sadly, looking for the words that would explain.

'I might not have been raised to be second in line to the throne, but I *was* raised a Svardian princess. It won't be easy, and I'll never be as good as my sister is, but I *love* Svardia. I am proud of our country and I would be honoured to represent them. My brother will be a fantastic ruler and I… I would never do anything to jeopardise that.' The truth and conviction ran through her soul, and sentiment and love raised goosebumps across her skin. 'So, yes. I do want to go back. I will *always* go back, no matter what, because my family and my country need me and I would never dishonour them.'

For the first time since meeting her Lykos realised the truth of Marit's royalty. There was nothing young or naïve about what she'd said, or even about her in that moment. It was a duty that, while she might not realise, suited her even if it demanded such a great sacrifice. A blush that had nothing to do with desire but was all about self-fulfilment lit her features and it was more devastating to his protective armour than even her touch. Her eyes sparkled with righteousness and assurance and he lost his breath.

'But if I'd said yes, what would you have done? Without Aleksander's shares?'

He wished he'd never told her. The fact that Kozlov's name was even in his thoughts at this table with her was abhorrent to him. 'I would have found a way,' he said truthfully.

'But how long would it have taken?'

Any number of years would have been worth it if Marit had wanted her freedom. Instead, he said, 'This is hardly appropriate date conversation.'

She smiled and his unease grew rather than diminished. 'Really? And what *would* be?' Marit asked, taking a sip of her drink, and he watched as her eyes grew round with unexpected pleasure. 'Oh.' The exclamation fell from her lips, making him think wicked thoughts. With ruthless determination he turned his focus on her question, realising that his experience was less of the date variety and more of the companion variety.

She arched an eyebrow, as if coming to the same conclusion about his experience and was about to tease him on it when in a panic he threw out words that surprised them both. 'I'd like to hear you play.'

The teasing expression on her face morphed into shock in an instant, and he could have cursed himself to hell and back.

'What?' she asked, her gaze locked on his even though he was sure that more than half her attention was actually on the piano.

'You play, don't you?' he asked, not quite sure why he was pursuing this, other than the awareness that her reaction made him even more convinced that it was the right thing to do.

She shook her head, even as she said, 'Yes.'

'Then I'd like to hear it.'

She looked at the table, hiding from his gaze. He was beginning to think he'd got it all wrong, when she raised her eyes to meet his and they were full of a yearning so pure that this time he really did lose his breath. It was as if he'd been punched right in the chest and he found that he was bracing himself in his seat just to stay upright.

'Really?'

He could see it. The disbelief that he'd want to hear her play. And he wanted to curse her entire family for making this woman doubt such a simple thing.

'More than anything else in the world.'

Lykos watched as Marit made her way to the piano. The musician seemed happy enough to let her play and, after a brief conversation between them, seemed eager to hear her too.

Lykos wasn't blind to the way the young man's gaze raked over her and he was forced to cage the proprietorial beast raging in his chest. But for a moment he saw Marit as the younger man did. Yes, there was a lightness to her, a youth, that was effervescent but not—as he had once told himself—naïve. There was also an experience that was beyond even his knowledge, the weight of inherent duty adding something to Marit that made him wonder how she'd kept that sense of fun and joy he'd witnessed in the park with the children and in the café in Milan; even in the boutique the shop assistant had seemed genuinely to turn towards her as if they were sunflowers and Marit was the sun.

She took a seat at the piano and swept a light touch across the keys with one hand and a smile curved her lips as if she were welcoming an old friend. Of the other few couples in the room, no one had seemed to notice, so lost were they in each other, making Lykos feel as if it were just the two of them. An intimacy strange for its publicness.

Suddenly he was hit by a wave of nervousness. Not because he thought she would be terrible, but he could see how important this was to her. He wanted it to go well because she needed it to go well. He clenched his jaw and swallowed. No matter what, he'd tell her that she was wonderful.

And then she started to play.

But what he hadn't expected was for her to sing.

Marit's fingers flew over the piano keys almost luxuriously, a series of notes that pulled at him and threw him into a song that filled him with a sense of old America and yearning. It was not what he'd expected and it made him stop and sit up.

Her voice was sultry and gentle as she sang about being at the end of one's life, a woman with her mother's name, building a world in his mind where people were trapped by life and helpless to fight against it. She sang of a desire like lightning that burned houses and he was enraptured.

And he felt it. The moment that everyone in the room stopped to listen. The sound of her voice and the piano raised the hairs on the back of his neck and poured longing, sadness, futility into his soul and his breath caught in his lungs.

She sang about the loss of youth, years passing and staying trapped and, even though she was conjuring images of rodeos and cowboys, he saw it—her future of missed opportunities and regret—and his heart turned for her, being stuck in a loveless marriage and wanting to be an angel that flew just as her voice spun into the room and beyond.

There were many times in his life that Lykos had felt trapped. He'd thrashed and raged against the cages of poverty and powerlessness. But what he saw in Marit was a woman who refused to let that trap be a cage, who instead welcomed it, embraced it, accepted it and allowed herself a freedom within it. How could he have ever thought her foolish or spoiled? How could he have ever dismissed her desire to become a musician as a petty whim when she *was* a musician down to her soul?

She was coming to the end of the song and he didn't want it to end. He could have listened to her for ever but, more than that, he knew if she stopped her song would come true. That this was her future. And he didn't want that for her. He wanted to take her away from it, to stop it from happening.

And as she drew her hands from the piano and placed them in her lap she turned to him and he saw it, the truth she had known from the very beginning and that he was only now understanding.

I will always go back, no matter what.

CHAPTER EIGHT

HER HEART WAS thundering in her chest. She'd never done that, never sung or performed in front of people before, and the moment of silence after she finished had her trembling on a precipice until the sincere clapping of the few people in the room broke into the quiet and drenched her in a happiness she'd never experienced before.

This was what she'd wanted for the young performers in the orchestra she worked with. That cresting shining wave, washing away all the nerves and all the fears of making a mistake or getting something wrong and basking in the light of being able to truly express themselves freely. Lykos had given her that. Something she'd feared she might never have. She wanted to tell him how much that meant to her, she wanted to thank him for bringing her dream to life.

And when she looked to him amongst the smiling faces in the room she found him sitting there, unmoving. For a moment she feared she'd done something wrong. But then she felt the sheer force of his gaze, the explosion of something between them that blocked out everything else. Her pulse pounded harder than it had done in the hotel room when she'd placed her palms on his chest. Heat flashed over her skin, making her feel cold and shivery and hot all at the same time.

And in that moment she realised for the first time that she wasn't alone in this feeling. That what she had seen was him fighting the same need, the same desire that swept over her like a tsunami. Its tide pulled at her feet as she made her way from the piano to their small table, threatening to push her this way and that. But it was his gaze that made her strong enough to make it, that filled her with a steely determination he must have seen in her eyes, because his gaze turned from speculative to assessing, even if he hid it behind the blink of an eye.

But it was too late. She had seen it. She had seen the extent of his need for her and she couldn't ignore or deny it any more. Plates of artfully catered food were placed on the table and she didn't break the connection of their gaze.

'You should eat.'

'I'm not hungry,' she declared. Not for food anyway. She didn't have to say it. The slight flare of his nostrils, the renewed determination in his eyes, the flex of the muscle at his jaw. Before, she would have seen rejection, a dismissive warning, but now she knew what they were—the evidence of how much he was fighting his reaction to her. Now, they were a red flag, encouraging and taunting.

She'd meant what she'd said. She would *always* return to Svardia to where she was needed, where she would finally prove herself. But she still had two days left and she couldn't stand the idea of living the rest of her life without knowing what it was like to feel his skin against hers. To know what it was like to kiss this powerful Greek billionaire and have him break his own armour for them to be together just for one night.

'I want to go home.'

'To Svardia?' he asked, purposely misunderstanding her meaning.

She narrowed her gaze at him and Lykos was instantly on guard. She shook her head very slowly, her gaze locked with his, and he felt hypnotised. Everything in him was fighting this. She was a princess. She was young. She did not know what she was doing, and certainly knew less of what she was asking for.

Because she *was* asking. Her unspoken request was as sure as any siren's call. And although she wasn't full of confidence and sensual experience like his previous bedfellows, she was so much more devastating than any of them.

'No.'

'No, what?'

'Marit,' he growled, the warning there in the depth and rumble of his voice. 'This is not a game.'

'I didn't think it was.'

'Then hear me when I say, *absolutely not*.'

Her eyes glinted in the low lighting, their food untouched, their drinks discarded.

'Tell me I'm wrong.'

'About what?'

'Tell me that you don't feel it. The attraction between us.'

He cursed. 'Of course I do. But that doesn't mean I have to act on it.'

'But what if I want to?'

'Consent works both ways, Princess.'

She reared back as if struck. 'You are accusing me of forcing myself on you?'

'No!' His harsh word cut through the softer ambience of the room. 'But I am not agreeing to this.'

She looked up at him, her eyes glistening, and for just a moment he thought her lip trembled, until the shutters came down and she nodded. 'Okay.' The word fell between them like a surrender and when she looked back up at him a mask was in place and it cut him deeper than he'd expected.

'Lykos, thank you for an enjoyable evening,' she said, 'but I am quite tired. It must have been the flight from Milan. And I didn't sleep well last...' her words trailed off, leaving memories of his migraine, of the way she'd unbuttoned his shirt, of the heat of her palms against his body to fill the space between them '...last night. If you wouldn't mind, I really would like to return to your house so that I can rest.'

A stubborn part of him wanted to refuse her request. Because it was wrong. Because he hadn't done this right. Because she'd asked for a date, her

first and perhaps only 'date' before she married a
stranger, and he'd failed. He'd given her an evening
that had ended in disappointment and hurt feelings
and he didn't like it. But neither would he force her
to stay. He had denied her once already—he couldn't
do it again.

He nodded finally and stood from the table. He
held his hand out to her more from habit than intent,
and he couldn't fault her for refusing it as she swept
from the room as regal as any queen. The car ride
back to Knightsbridge was just as bad. A silence
that nudged and jolted his conscience every time the
car turned or stopped at a set of lights. She was so
quiet he couldn't hear her breathe and it was only the
whiteness of the knuckles on her fisted hands that
showed any kind of emotion.

He wanted to explain. He wanted to comfort her.
But what use were his words when he wouldn't act
on them? Far better for her to think him an unfeeling
bastard than to admit…what? That he feared touching her? That kissing her would be his downfall?
Because, in truth, he wasn't sure that he'd be able to
ever let her go? That it wasn't her that he was trying
to protect, but himself?

He cursed out loud and she flinched, but before he
could apologise they pulled up beside his home and,
without waiting for the driver, Marit slipped from
the car and out into the night. He took his time getting out of the car, in the hope that he could control
himself before he did something drastic like reach

for her and draw her to him. The thought put images into his mind that began to unravel his willpower.

She was waiting by the front door and he had to reach around her to place his thumb on the security pad of the house. The sound of the lock releasing cut into the night and Marit pushed at the door to escape him. She was halfway to the staircase by the time he closed the door behind him. He couldn't leave it like this. He couldn't let her go thinking… He cursed. He couldn't even imagine what she was thinking. He needed to let her go.

'Marit.'

The word erupted unbidden from his lips, stopping her dead in her tracks, but she refused to turn to look at him. He wanted to make sure she was okay, he needed to see that she was.

He closed the distance between them, his hungry gaze raking over the dress that clung to her skin. His eyes swept down her back as his hands wanted to do and snagged on the way the material clung to her hips, the curve of her backside, the tops of her thighs… His gaze flicked back up to shoulders that were stiff with tension and cut to hands that were fisted.

'Marit.' This time her name was a plea as he caught her wrist and turned her to him, instantly regretting it the moment he saw the tears gathered in her eyes.

He reached up to cup her jaw, his thumb gently grazing her cheekbone, sweeping up to snare the lone tear that had fallen as she'd closed her eyes to prevent him from seeing her pain. Angry words and hot demands he could deflect and reject, but the hurt, the pain he'd seen glittering there? It was the final blow to his defences and he knew in that moment that he would lay himself bare for her and still be there when she walked away from him.

Her eyelashes glistened with unshed tears as she prised them open to cast him with such a look that he felt turned to stone.

'What can I do?' he demanded, his voice ragged and full of gravel, bringing his other hand up to frame her face.

She speared her bottom lip with her teeth and, unable to help himself, his thumb dropped to her lips and gently prised it free from its ivory cage. She raised her eyes to his and placed her hand on his wrist at the side of her face to hold him to her when he might pull away.

'I know I can't ask for more, I know that is impossible, but please. Let me have what little I can.'

Lykos felt the whispered words against his skin, sinking deep into his body, his soul.

'You deserve more than *a little*, Marit, you deserve *everything*.'

'I don't want what you think I deserve. I want you.'

The simple words stripped a layer from the walls he'd placed between himself and his princess. He searched her eyes, looking for doubt, looking for uncertainty, but all he saw was naked pleading and she should never have had to beg.

'No more,' he whispered to himself.

'What?'

'I will fight you no more,' he said, just before he lowered his head and swept his lips across hers.

The feel of his lips against hers swept all her concerns away: fear that he would reject her, that he didn't want her. It was too close to how everyone else treated her, but Lykos was different. This Lykos, his lips claiming hers, was everything. Marit knew what she was asking for, despite her practical innocence. But to enter a loveless marriage without ever knowing the intimate touch of affection would be a tragedy to someone who felt so much.

When Lykos touched her she felt *alive*. Alive in a way she'd only felt when she was playing the piano. It was as if she were the musical instrument that sang beneath his deft fingers, strings vibrating and trembling, a tone so pure, so true and clear, that it was a siren's call, weaving a spell that affected them both equally.

His tongue swept across her lips, teasing her until she opened for him and, *oh…*

As Lykos took possession of the kiss all rational thought stopped and Marit succumbed to pure sensation. His tongue danced with hers, pulling a crescendo from deep within her, rushing towards some seemingly impossible conclusion. His hands cradled her face and she leaned into the gentle cage, wanting to feel him against her skin everywhere. Her heart fluttered in her throat as if wanting to escape her body and fly to his.

Her hands slipped beneath his jacket to the breadth of his shoulders, his skin hot beneath her palms through the soft cotton of his shirt. She clung to him, to the muscles rippling beneath her touch, and realised just how much he was holding himself back. And she didn't want him to hold back. She wanted him as Lykos. Unleashed, powerful, demanding and challenging. Everything that people around her thought she was unworthy of, or too delicate for.

She pushed his jacket from his shoulders, neither caring where it fell, and her hands swept down, over biceps and elbows to a waist corded with muscle, and pulled the shirt free of his belt. They'd done this before, the echo of déjà vu pulsing between them, making Lykos pull back from the kiss and study her once again.

Marit felt the loss keenly and almost followed him back as he leaned from the reach of her lips, but he soothed the loss by sweeping his hand from her cheek to rest it against the thunderous beating of her heart. The gentle pressure was reassuring and comforting in a way that was nothing to do with the sensual play between them and spoke of something deeper, something lasting, no matter how little time they had to share together.

'*Latriea mou,*' he whispered, the lyricism of his words building a rhythm in her soul that she'd never forget. He shook his head, his eyes raking over her as if disbelieving of what he saw and, for the first

●

time, Marit didn't doubt that it was *her*. That he was cherishing, relishing and wondering purely at *her*. It was an intoxicating feeling, one she could quickly become addicted to if she were not careful.

'Are you sure that this is what you want, *agápi mou*?'

She nodded but, seeing the pleading look in his eyes, put her intent to words. 'Absolutely.'

'If you change your mind, if you want to stop for any reason—' Marit was already shaking her head, but again he gave her a look that warned her, *wanted* her, to take this seriously. That he cared more for her needs than any discomfort of his own meant too much to her. She didn't know what to do with that, so she closed the distance between them and drew his bottom lip between her teeth and nipped him gently, quickly soothing the sting with a sweep of her tongue.

Shock and surprise were evident on his face for about two seconds before desire lit his eyes like fireworks and he plundered her mouth with his own. Marit lost her breath and her mind to the kiss. For what felt like hours she drowned in exquisite sensation. The way his tongue teased and taunted, his lips bringing moans of want and cries of need from her mouth, his hands leaving her face to mould a body that rose to his touch, as if she were a marionette and he held her strings—the connection between them invisible but too tangible not to be real. Marit felt as if she'd been living a half-life until his touch.

Frustration began to unspool within her, twisting

and turning from her core, making her hot and un-settled. She wanted their clothes gone, she wanted him against her, her body's primal reaction to him instinctive and urgent. This time she drew the kiss to an end, shifting her thighs together and the heat of impatience stinging her cheeks. She didn't know how to ask for what she wanted. She *heard* it, a whole string quartet played in her mind of what she wanted Lykos to do to her, to do *with* her. But the words…

She felt his eyes rake over her assessingly and then at the same time they both said, 'Bedroom.'

Marit couldn't help the laugh that bubbled up, cutting through the frustration and building something softer, sweeter, but no less needy between them. As if he'd come to a decision, Lykos nodded to himself in that way of his and swept her up into his arms, marching them up the staircase of his townhouse towards the floor where she had got dressed earlier that evening. But instead of turning into the guest suite Lykos pressed forward and they entered his room, his footsteps slowing, his eyes only for her as he shifted his hold so that she could stand on her own two feet again, but still within the circle of his hold.

Once again, his hand rose to cup her jaw. His eyes flashed silver in the dark room. Two large sash windows displayed a magnificent London skyline, but Marit wouldn't look away for the world.

'*Kardiá mou*, Marit…' He seemed as unable as she was to be without touch or contact for long—as if they knew how little time they had to share and couldn't, wouldn't, waste a moment of it. 'I wish you could see what I see,' he said between the kisses he pressed to her lips, her throat, her collarbone, following the pattern his fingers traced across her skin.

Her hands clung to his waist, pulling him to her, relishing the feel of the power and length of him against her body and finally, when he leaned back, she had enough room to sneak her hands between them. Quick fingers made light work of the buttons on his shirt and she spread his shirt apart and slipped it from his shoulders, all the while unable to remove her gaze from his chest. Her palms itched to feel the swirls of dark hair covering the clearly defined muscles that spoke not of hours in the gym but pure raw masculinity and power.

She could feel the weight of his gaze as he watched her taking him in, the depth of his curiosity, but, drawn back to him by that invisible string, she pressed kisses to his chest and thought she heard him groan, felt it in her core. Downward her kisses went, but when she reached the snap on his trousers he gently pulled her away, turning her in his arms so that she faced the windows and a large standing mirror in the corner of the room.

'It's my turn,' he whispered as he kissed just beneath her ear, sending a shiver of sparks over her body and pebbling nipples already teased and needy. Her breath stuttered in her chest as he swept her hair over one shoulder, his fingers finding the barely visible zip at the back of the dress and slowly, ever so slowly, drew the tab downwards. In the mirror she could see that his eyes followed the path of the zip and his hands, relished the slight flush beneath the tan of his skin, the way his lips had parted slightly as if so utterly consumed by what he was seeing he'd given up all self-awareness. Marit took all that in and more.

The way her own eyes hungrily devoured him, the way her body responded to his, standing taller, prouder, empowered by his need. That his arousal and desire would feed her own was something she never could have expected or imagined. She bit her lip and in the mirror saw wantonness and need. She saw not the loss of innocence but the gain of something wondrous and her heart sank the moment she realised that she couldn't keep this, couldn't keep *him*.

Without a title, he would never have a place in her future and in that second she knew she would never have the chance to feel loved for ever. The only thing that kept her standing was the knowledge that she would take this moment with her, and it made her bold when she might not have been otherwise, made her determined when she might have conceded power. Lykos met her gaze in the mirror and she could feel the question hanging in the air, before she shrugged the dress from her shoulders and bared herself to him.

Lykos would have cursed if he'd been capable of speech. She had turned him to stone and it was a moment he would remember for the rest of his life. She watched him taking her in and it was the most erotic thing he'd ever experienced, hardening his erection to the point of near pain. Holding himself back became a physical thing, his jaw clenched, hands fisted to stop him from bruising her with his need. She met his gaze in the mirror before turning to him, a bare inch between them and she felt painfully out of his reach. Until she closed the distance and her chest pressed against his, her thighs, the juncture of them, meeting the hardened length of him through the trousers he still wore.

Then he noticed the hesitancy in her eyes and the bottom fell from his world.

'What is it, *agápi mou*?' he whispered, her cheek fitting into his palm as if she'd been made for him. She bit her lip and his thumb soothed it free again. She looked away as if unable to say what she wanted and he hated that. Hated that she feared his response. Didn't she know that he'd give her anything that she asked?

When she looked back up at him, determination, need and something very close to fury blazed in her eyes. She had morphed into a phoenix, traces of the defiant runaway Princess twisted into strength and power, and it was incredible.

'Make me yours so that no one can ever take that away.'

It was as if the leash holding him back had been cut and all the desire, all the need, all the *feelings* he'd held back for so long rushed to the forefront and overwhelmed him completely. He walked her backwards to the bed and she relished it, her eyes delighting in his power and his desire for her.

He kissed her and guided her back against the pillows of the bed, her body instinctively opening for him as he leaned on one hand and used the other to trace the curves of her body, her skin like satin beneath his palm, shivering and trembling with need as he smoothed his way over the curve of her waist, hip, sweeping around to the inside of her soft thighs, pulling the thong from her body, spreading her legs and delving into the blonde curls damp from her desire.

Her body arched as he parted her with his fingers and a moan of pleasure mixed with an intake of breath. He watched every minute of it, utterly undone by Marit's rapture. He lost himself in it for an infinity, the gold and jade shards in her eyes on fire, the pink flush of her cheeks and the hitch in her breath as she climbed closer and closer to her orgasm.

Her body undulated with the shift of his hands and tension corded her as he delved deeper into her with a finger, gently testing her muscles, readying her so as to make it as least painful as possible. In a heartbeat that tension rolled into a wave of ecstasy and he could have died then, the happiest he had ever been. Believed even that he might have found his life's purpose, and then she opened her eyes and pinned him with a gaze so hot that he felt branded to his very soul.

Her hand reached down to circle his forearm, the sight of her slender fingers wrapped around him pushing him towards the edge of feral.

'Lykos,' she said, his name a plea he could no longer deny. He leaned back from her only long enough to remove his trousers and underwear, casting them away with ruthless efficiency and returning to her, bracing on his forearms, his hands once again cradling her cheeks.

'I have been told that this will hurt. Not terribly—'

'Lykos,' Marit replied, her voice husky from her pleasure. 'I've had the birds and the bees talk,' she teased. But not too much, he could see what it meant, his concern for her. 'I want this. I want it to be with you.'

Her words did something to him that he wouldn't, couldn't look at now. Instead, he reached into the nightstand and removed a condom from the drawer, silently vowing to make this as pleasurable for Marit as possible. He rolled the latex over himself and settled between her legs, his erection pulsing with restrained need, and slowly, so incredibly slowly, he joined with her.

A pleasure so sublime it hurt his heart filled him as he filled her, never once taking his eyes from hers, never missing a single moment of her response to his intrusion. He felt the moment she experienced her pain, the tension and stiffness around him making him stop instantly while she adjusted to the new experience, saw the moment the shock left her eyes and was replaced by wonder. Shifting beneath him, moving at first for comfort and then an instinctive search for pleasure, more and more as her hips rolled beneath him. Every moment as wondrous for him as it was for her.

Finally turning to him, her eyes now full of questions. 'Is it always like this?' Her whispered words were full of awe.

He wouldn't lie to her. 'No,' he replied, his heart in his words. 'It is never like this, *agápi mou.*'

There was no misunderstanding, no confusion between them. He wouldn't allow it. She could see how much this meant to him, because he too had laid himself bare for her. It was an intimacy he had never allowed anyone. And when she reached up to cup his jaw he knew she could see the truth of it.

Slowly he began to move, Marit's body instinctively arching into his, her head falling back against the pillow, the golden strands of her hair fanning out like a halo. Again and again he pushed them to the brink and back, drenching her in pleasure and drowning in her cries until neither of them could take any more and, with one last thrust, Lykos launched them into a sea of ecstasy, leaving them to drift on currents that sent ripples through their bodies for long hours after.

The sound of Lykos's phone ringing woke them as the sun's early morning rays were filtering in through the sash windows of the room. Having only just closed his eyes after making love to Marit again, he groaned in frustration, eliciting a gentle laugh from the half-asleep Princess next to him.

'Aren't you going to answer it?'

'No, I'm going to hope that they get the message and go away,' he grumped into the pillow, muffling the words and sounding like the kind of carefree youth he had never been.

She turned her head and pierced him with shards of gold and green and tease and his heart turned. He'd never seen anyone so beautiful. And then the phone rang again, ruining the moment. Marit's gentle giggles turned into a laugh and Lykos snared the phone and barked, *'Nai?'* without taking his eyes from her once.

'Lykos? It's Theron. I need you to come to Greece. Right now.'

CHAPTER NINE

MARIT HAD NEVER seen Lykos like this. Angry? Yes. Frustrated? Aroused? Yes.

She bit her lip to stop herself from raising her fingers to her mouth in memory of last night, in *wonder* of what they had shared. A part of her knew that it would have been easier to resign herself to her future if she had not known, not experienced, just what it was that she would be denying herself.

Love.

No. She shook her head. She might have been innocent last night but she was not naïve. She wasn't in love with him and, as she looked at Lykos, she knew he would never feel that way about her. She cared for him a great deal—of course she did, she wouldn't have been able to give herself to him as she had done last night if she did not. But…love? No. Marit had spent her entire life looking for love, one way or another. The moment she had gone to Paris to marry, she had put such thoughts and such desire from her mind and heart for ever.

But when she saw the dark bruises beneath

Lykos's eyes, the muscle flexed at his jaw, she knew that she would do anything to ease his fear if she could.

'Theron didn't say anything other than that he needed you in Greece?'

'*Óchi.*' He shook his head. 'He said he had to go. That Summer needed him. If something has happened to Katy, their little baby girl—'

Marit reached across the space between her seat and his, anchored by the seatbelt needed for the private jet's descent into Athens. That he didn't shake her off was sign enough to Marit that this man who, by all accounts, considered himself an island, untouchable and above the connections of the mere mortals around him was scared, *terrified*, for his friends.

Disembarking the plane happened in the blink of an eye, a sleek black town car waited for them on the runway, chauffeured by a suited man in dark glasses and a set jaw. Through the entire journey to their destination Lykos's knee bounced against one fisted hand, the other tightly wrapped in Marit's. She knew better than to assure a man with Lykos's life experience that it would all be okay. Instead, she became the silent support she instinctively knew he needed.

They pulled up to a house and the sight of other cars lining the grand estate did absolutely nothing to ease the tension racing through each of them—as if they were now connected on a level Marit didn't yet comprehend. The car stopped opposite the front door, Lykos only releasing Marit's hand to leave the confines of the car and vault up the steps to the door, where he paused as if bracing himself for what he might find. Marit slipped behind him, her hand on his back, and finally his fist fell on the door.

What happened next was so confusing it took Marit a moment to sort through it all.

A tall, dark-haired Greek with a broad smile opened the door to demand what had taken Lykos so long. Behind him was the sound of a party in full swing, the happiness and bright sunshine utterly at odds with the drama of Marit and Lykos's desperate journey here at dawn, fearing the worst.

Beside him was a small but utterly beautiful woman with a tiny baby held preciously in her arms. The woman seemed to realise what had happened much more quickly than her partner—which Marit guessed by the way that she reached out to slap his arm.

'Theron, I *told* you he would think the worst,' she scolded angrily in English.

'What? No, I just knew he wouldn't come otherwise,' Theron Thiakos said happily to his wife, until he finally caught sight of the expression on Lykos's face. 'Ach, *sygnómi*, Lykos.' Summer, from what Lykos had told Marit about Theron and his partner, looked between her partner and his friend and, cradling the baby with one hand, pulled Lykos into a firm hug with the other.

'Lykos, he's an unthinking beast. I'm so sorry,' she said.

'Does that mean you've come to your senses and will finally leave the *maláka* for me?' Lykos teased.

Marit could have had whiplash from the change in Lykos's tone. Summer seemed equally suspicious, but Theron was instantly put at ease. Neither was Marit fooled by the teasing, bold flirtation, having experienced the real thing the night before.

'That's my woman,' growled Theron.

'I am no one's woman, thank you very much,' Summer replied in English. 'Please ignore these brutes,' she said, playfully swatting them both on the arm—even though there was something softer when she looked at Lykos. She introduced herself and their little baby girl Katy—short for Catherine—and brought them into the beautiful villa.

'Why the cloak and dagger?' Lykos asked in English for the benefit of Summer and Marit.

'We didn't think you'd come,' Summer explained.

They looked between Summer and her husband until Theron said, 'Kyros is here.'

A swift sharp nod preceded a clenched jaw. 'Of course. He is your father. I wouldn't have expected anything less.' The shoulder shrug should have dismissed their concerns but it only raised Marit's curiosity, until she linked the name with the father figure who had betrayed Lykos.

'Which is why I expected you to find an excuse not to come,' Theron clarified, cutting through Marit's thoughts.

'Fair,' Lykos admitted, seemingly good-naturedly.

'That's what I thought. See?' He turned to Summer. 'Told you.'

Summer bumped shoulders with her partner and turned back to Marit. 'Forgive me for staring, but you do look quite familiar. Have we met?'

It took ten minutes to talk Summer down from her panic at having a princess at their party and then another ten to assure her that they didn't have to follow any particular rules of etiquette. Marit, as if sensing the broiling mass of emotions swirling like petrol in his stomach, drew Summer and Theron into a conversation about Katy—which would give Lykos anywhere from five to twenty minutes to get himself under control.

He pulled at his cufflinks and flexed his hand, opening and closing it to restore circulation to his fingers. His pulse was still wildly out of control, not that anyone would know to look at him. He had found himself in a quiet corner of the estate, in the garden overlooking the Aegean Sea, a sight that had always calmed him in the past.

The rays of the midday sun beat down on his skin, familiar and welcoming. It was a ridiculous sentiment, but one he couldn't shake. A London sun could be painfully harsh or frustratingly weak. Hong Kong's was humid, damp, and for Lykos was too close to the skin. But here it was *home*.

But even such serene thoughts did nothing to diminish the pounding at his temple. It was too soon for another migraine, surely. He ran his palm over the stubble on his jaw, not having had time to shave when he'd come here thinking the worst.

Christé mou, he'd thought something had happened to Katy. Fear and frustration had pounded through him all the way here. And now that he knew Katy was fine, his pulse still raced. Concern still edged at his awareness and he could no longer ignore why.

In ten years he'd amassed a fortune that would have made his father weep and Kyros blink. He'd dominated financial markets, his name whispered in the wealthiest of circles. He had apartments all over the world, and a woman whenever he wanted...

But none of them had made him feel anything like what he had experienced last night with Marit. And she was the one woman he would never be allowed to keep. She was one thing that no amount of money, no amount of apparent respectability could attain. Marit must return to Svardia so that she could be married off to some titled noble, as Svardian legislation decreed. Lykos let out a bitter laugh. No matter how much money he'd made, or what he'd achieved in the time since he'd left Kyros, it *still* wasn't enough.

His gut churned as he remembered that in exchange for taking Marit home he would receive Aleksander's shares. The thought made him feel nauseous. As if the night he had spent with Marit had payment. He'd meant what he'd said in London. If she wanted to escape, if she wanted her freedom, he would do everything in his power to make it happen.

I will always go back.

Something about the way she'd said it had reminded him of his mother and it had cut deeper, and darker, than he could ever have imagined. In his mind's eye, he saw his mother's large glistening eyes, the feel of her palm against his cheek.

The only way I'll be safe is if he can never use you against me again. So don't look for me. Don't come for me.

And he couldn't shake the feeling that when Marit left his life, this time he would be even more alone.

A cold sweat at his nape turned icy with a fresh blast of salty air, anchoring him in the present. When he felt a presence behind him he could have sworn that somehow the past was repeating itself.

Kyros came to stand beside him, less than a foot between them and closer than they'd been in over ten years. A silent roar of rage built inside of Lykos, thrashing and snarling and wanting out, the hurt from too many things in his past colliding in this one moment, but he had too much control to do so. Instead, the world would have seen two old friends perhaps, in a shared moment.

'You've done incredibly well for yourself, Lykos.'

'Yes, I have. But if you think for one moment your acknowledgement of that fact means anything to me then you are sorely mistaken.' His pulse throbbed painfully in a throat that felt thick and sore.

'I did you a great disservice when I asked you—'

'*Sent me.*'

Kyros surrendered a sigh. '*Sent you,*' the old man confirmed, 'after Mariam.'

Lykos felt the weight of the blue-eyed gaze on his cheeks. Was Kyros taking in the changes that time had wrought, as Lykos had done in Norfolk a few months ago? He hadn't liked how shaken he'd been to see the larger-than-life vibrant man from his youth with wrinkles, shocking white hair and a sadness in his eyes that had been for more than the loss of Althaia, his wife.

'Lykos, I didn't know. I had no idea that Mariam had a child.'

'Why did you do it then? Why did you send me after her? What were you hoping to achieve? You had a wife, Agyros. She was sick and you had been with another woman.'

'What drew me to Mariam—and Mariam to me—is between us,' Kyros growled, the roar of an old tiger not yet done with the world. Inside, grief and hurt twisted in Lykos's heart. 'I told Althaia as soon as it had happened. But I shouldn't have done it and I certainly shouldn't have used you to track Mariam down. Lykos, even then, in a way I cannot explain, I loved both women. I thought that perhaps now you might finally understand how far we will go for the women we love…but perhaps not.'

Lykos's jaw ached from how tightly he had clenched it. Kyros's gaze burned into him and it took everything in his power not to react.

'That, however, is not what I wanted to say.'

'Oh, really? There's more?' Lykos cursed himself, knowing how childish he sounded, but he felt out of control, wild and frantic. *This was what happened when you let emotions in, he warned himself. This was what happened when you let Marit in.*

Kyros was frowning, as if finally sensing the unease within him. The old man went to place a hand on his shoulder. 'Lykos—'

Lykos shook him off before the touch could connect and it seemed Kyros decided to keep whatever he'd been about to say to himself.

Kyros's sigh seemed weary and weighted, even to Lykos's ears. 'No matter what has passed and what may come to pass in the future, if you allow it, I owe you an apology. I should never have asked you to do that. And I know that I let you down. I am sincerely sorry for that, Lykos.'

Lykos didn't know how to respond. He'd spent so many years being angry at this man, resenting him and hating him sometimes. But now that he'd received the Kyros's apology it didn't quite mean what he'd thought it would.

'It will take time, Lykos, but I promise you I'll show you that I mean what I say. Having my daughter in my life...it has changed so much. And it's reminded me of what I've missed. With you. But I understand if that's not what you want. Just...' Kyros seemed to run out of the energy that had driven him this far '...just keep it in mind.'

Kyros waited and after a beat longer than he'd probably expected, and less than Lykos had planned, he nodded, surrendering to a desire that he thought he'd buried a long time ago. A desire for family, for a home.

* * *

Marit watched Lykos with an older man who, she realised, was Kyros. She'd tried to look away, to give them the privacy they deserved, but she'd been too worried about Lykos. He'd brushed off Theron's trick easily enough, but Marit hadn't been fooled. From what Lykos had told her, being here would be incredibly difficult. Confronting Kyros? Inconceivable. Summer sat opposite her rocking Katy, unable to hide the glances she also sent in their direction.

'So, how long have you known Lykos?' Summer asked, making it sound like more than just polite conversation. The warmth in her was apparent, putting Marit at ease almost instantly. She reminded Marit a little of her sister Freya and the thought stung a little more than it should.

In the last few years they'd not spoken as often as they once had, with Marit unable to hide the resentment at the loss of Freya's attention as she took on her royal duties. At the time it had reminded her too much of her parents. But now, faced with the same position, Marit *understood*. She understood each member of her family a little more. Understood the purpose and the bone-deep willingness to serve their country, making it hurt to think how selfishly and childishly she'd behaved. It was as if somehow, being seen by Lykos, *feeling* seen by him had enabled her to see herself more clearly. She shook the thought off, trying to find her way back to answering Summer's question.

'It feels like a lifetime,' she answered, unsure how

the other woman would react to the news that they'd only known each other a matter of days. But as she said the words she felt them as the truth. Only it was a different lifetime to the one that lay ahead of her, or even behind her, as if she had been allowed to slip into a parallel world before stepping up to do her duty.

'He is a complicated man,' Summer observed of Lykos.

'Do you think so?' Marit couldn't help but ask.

'You don't?' she asked with a smile.

As if drawn once again by that invisible thread, she felt the tug as he approached the table, the shadows in his eyes masked by the softness in his gaze as it focused on Katy and he pressed a kiss to the baby's cheek once he reached the table. Marit was surprised when his hand reached out to her shoulder and she couldn't have stopped herself from anchoring it there with her own. Summer's eyes took in the small gesture and smiled. Marit looked up at Lykos as he turned to her, the question in her eyes answered by his. They would talk later.

'Ah, there you are,' Theron said. 'I've been looking for you everywhere.'

'Really, Theron. You are old enough to go to the toilet by yourself these days,' Lykos teased.

'Well, it's just that I might need your help to hold—'

Marit coughed as air got caught in her throat and Summer cried her outrage, slapping her husband and drawing curious gazes from the guests.

'When will you two behave?' Summer demanded.

'Never,' they both replied, before breaking into wide genuine grins. For the first time since arriving, Marit felt something ease in her chest and she took in the powerful bond between the three. It was full of love, affection and trust and for a moment she allowed herself to feel a tendril of grief that she would never be able to be a part of that. No. Her future lay in Svardia with another man and another set of duties.

The rest of the afternoon passed in easy conversation and delicious food. Lykos spent a long while followed around by a group of children. One clung to his leg, one to his arm and another tried desperately to climb onto his back. Not surprised in the least, it warmed Marit's heart to see him so gentle and patient with them. She saw him whisper to a girl who looked about sixteen, who ran off eagerly to do his bidding, but Theron took the chair beside her and distracted her.

Eventually Lykos relaxed enough to exchange a civil conversation with Kyros—bringing so much happiness to Summer that Marit knew exactly why both men were trying so hard to fix something that had caused so much pain. Lykos might tease and taunt, might charm and flirt his way through his exchanges, but now that she had seen through the mask, seen the truth that he hid from the world, she would never be able to not see it.

The mask was a shadow, a mirage, protecting a man who had so much love to give but had never been allowed to. His father had abused it, his mother had refused it, Kyros had betrayed it and Theron had rejected it, *before* their reunion.

'What is it, *agápi mou*?'

'Mm?' Marit asked, leaning into the palm of his hand.

'What has you looking so sad?'

She couldn't tell him. Because the answer had surprised her so much it had stopped her tongue. Instead, she forced a smile to her lips and simply said that she was tired.

'I will make our goodbyes. But, before we do, I have something for you.'

His eyes twinkled irresistibly, their silver sparks drawing her gaze rather than what he held in his hand. Finally she looked down and when she realised what it was she gasped.

'A tattoo!' she cried.

'A *temporary* one,' he clarified, referring to the silver transfer in an ornate pattern.

The detail was beautiful and that he'd thought, even now, of the list she'd written back in Milan—a list that she'd never thought he'd take seriously—it meant so much to her. She put the temporary tattoo into her bag, realising that she would never use it. It would, instead, be locked away with her most prized possessions, as a reminder of the kindness she'd once been given by a Greek billionaire.

Within ten minutes Lykos had extricated them from the throng at Theron and Summer's party with Marit having had her cheeks pinched only a few times. Lykos fared worse, or at least seemed to. There was a lot of shouting in Greek and gestures that ranged from warm to aggressively affectionate. A handshake between him and Kyros was more than anyone had expected and it was clearly a sign of hope to so many.

'Are you really tired? Or were you just ready to leave?' he asked as they closed the door to Theron and Summer's gorgeous villa.

She bit her lip and turned to him.

'Thank you,' he mouthed exaggeratedly and pressed a swift kiss to her lips that seemed to take them both by surprise. Lykos cleared his throat and Marit turned away to hide her smile. 'Are you happy to walk?' he asked. When she nodded, he threw his jacket to the driver and dismissed him for the rest of the day.

They turned onto a street but Marit couldn't have described it, instead her attention was caught by the way Lykos removed his cufflinks, putting them in his pocket before rolling up his sleeves. She thought at first what had caught her attention was the sight of his powerful forearms, but after a while she realised what it was; she had never seen him so relaxed. Only with them gone did she realise how many times she'd seen him pull on his cufflinks as if in the habit of checking everything was 'just so'.

She tucked the thought away the moment Lykos took her hand in his and instead, with the constant awareness of how little time they had left, she chose to enjoy the moment, finding something peaceful in walking beside him. Even more when he let go of her hand and drew her beneath his arm, tucking her into his side as if they both wished that she could stay there.

A shuddering sigh vibrated through his body. 'He apologised.'

'Kyros?' she asked, though she was sure that was the answer.

Lykos nodded. 'I don't… I don't know what to do with it.'

She tried to imagine what it would be like to hear an apology from her parents and realised that she never would. Everything they had done was for Svardia and if Marit confronted them with the hurts of her childhood, Svardia would be their answer and she couldn't argue with that. It was sad that it had taken being *needed*, being given that responsibility, to finally understand what it was like to go against the heart's wishes for duty. But maybe her parents had gone against their own wishes too. Maybe Kyros had and only now was able to admit it.

'Perhaps,' Marit said, thinking of how much time she'd needed even to begin to feel some kind of peace with her hurts, 'you don't have to do anything with it yet. Maybe you need time just to feel it?'

He stopped and pulled her to stand before him. 'Can I kiss you?'

Love blazed in her heart for this man and she promised that even though they could never have a future, this would be what she took with her. 'For the next two days, you don't have to ask.' She pulled him to her and the kiss burned from sweet to almost indecent in a heartbeat.

'Perhaps we should find your apartment,' Marit teased.

'Soon. There's something I want to show you before we do.'

Curious, and a little excited, she searched the length of the cobbled street he'd brought her to. There were boutiques and coffee shops on either side of the street, but nothing that she could tell as being special. A knowing smile curved Lykos's lips as he pulled her towards a small wooden door she had missed completely.

Frowning, he drew her across the threshold and down a set of stairs. As they reached the bottom of the stairs, the dark underground room opened up and she saw a bar on one side and small tables opposite. The place was packed, the smell of wine and something sweet, and there were so many conversations going on that it made her feel deliciously anonymous rather than overwhelmed. But beneath it all she heard something that made her look towards the corner of the taverna where a man sat on a dais. A quick peal of notes rippled over the chatter and soon the audience quietened. Lykos watched her with a smile and she knew somehow that this was what he'd wanted her to see.

'What instrument is that? It sounds like a mandolin, but…lower in pitch?' she hedged.

'It is a bouzouki.'

Listening intently, she didn't realise that she'd pulled them through the mass of people, leading

Lykos by the hand until she stood at the front, watching the man on the small dais, his foot resting on a block and a long-necked instrument in his lap, his fingers flying across the metal strings. Marit marvelled at the stillness of his body and the incredible flight of notes that poured into the air between them.

Lykos drew her against his chest as they listened, his arms enfolding her. He dipped his head to her ear and, keeping his voice low, told her how he and Theron used to sneak in here when they were teenagers. He explained that the music was called *rebetiko*. In words that raised goosebumps on her skin, he told her that it was the music of the underground, favoured by the country's *undesirables*. Many of the songs had been subject to censorship for a time because the lyrics spoke of alcohol, drugs, and were politically disruptive.

As Lykos spoke to her of the music's history the song morphed and the cycling chords drew foot taps from the crowd, growing loud enough to become the song's heartbeat. Claps soon joined in and somehow the music took on the weight of an orchestra, as if everyone present had a part to play in the production of the music. And, above it all, the trembling melody spun higher in a pitch that wound in her heart until she felt a burning against the backs of her eyes. She felt the rebelliousness of the song in her soul, the expression of frustration and fight similar to that of blues, but different. There was a yearning to *rebetiko* music that felt strangely just out of her grasp. As if she were so close to understanding it, to feeling it, but also knowing that it was something she would never be able to hold.

She began to sway in Lykos's arms just as some of the crowd pulled back from a man, arms outstretched and clicking his fingers in time with the claps and foot taps. His hat, looking like something from the thirties, was at a downward angle, his face partially hidden as he swayed from side to side, his footsteps surprisingly light for the circular steps he was making. There was a grace that reminded her of flamenco dancers, but heavier, grounded, deeper and so much part of the music that the dancer and musician became inseparable.

'Are your feet hurting yet?' Lykos whispered into her ear beneath the trill of the music she had half fallen in love with.

'What?' she asked, momentarily confused.

'Your list,' Lykos whispered in her ear as she wondered whether she and Lykos might have also become inseparable. 'You wanted to go to a concert. And this is the best one I've ever been to.'

'And dance until my feet hurt,' she remembered.

He looked down at her, and the words sat on her tongue, waiting for her to speak them. Waiting for her to tell him that she loved him. But she couldn't. She just couldn't be another person who claimed they loved him and walked away. So instead she kissed him with all the words that she couldn't say, she kissed him with such passion that the crowd around them began to laugh and whistle and, smiling into one last kiss, Lykos took her home.

CHAPTER TEN

LYKOS WOKE WITH a start. It was not a gentle way to do so. His pulse raced, his breath was rapid in his chest, as if someone had fired a starting gun and not told him that he was in the race. He looked to where Marit should have been in the bed beside him and saw that it was empty. Panic fired through him, even though he was sure she was still in the apartment, because he saw in an instant that this was how he would wake every morning for the rest of his life. Knowing that something was horribly wrong, because she would never be there next to him.

It was only when he caught sight of her on the balcony that looked out onto the azure blue of the Aegean that his breath slowed, even if his heart didn't. She was wearing one of his shirts—the blue cotton dwarfed her and billowed around her thighs in the early morning breeze. The blonde jagged twists of her hair fell around her shoulders, making him want to sweep them aside and press kisses to her shoulder blades. And then he realised why he was so disorientated.

He had slept. He had slept not only through Marit waking up, but he didn't remember anything after bringing her to the bedroom last night. But he never slept.

In all the years since he'd been on the streets he would pace his way through the night hours. He had never felt comfortable in a bed. As if he didn't trust the softness of it. Never stopped expecting it to bite him or be taken away. He racked his brain. He'd not had a drink yesterday at Theron's party, not with so many people around and not with Kyros.

I let you down. I am sincerely sorry for that.

Kyros's apology whispered into the morning. He still didn't know what to do with it. Those words had recalled a part of him he'd thought he'd buried so deep he'd never have to face it again. It made him feel unsettled and disorientated, but also in the midst of all of that was a core of stillness. A moment that made him felt *heard*, that made him felt *seen*.

And he began to understand what Marit had been trying to do by marrying the Frenchman. To avoid being tied to another person in her life who didn't see what she needed, what she loved, what she was so damn good at that he wanted the world to see it too. A new fresh pain sliced into his heart then. In doing her duty by returning to Svardia, Marit was knowingly sacrificing her soul's needs for her country and her family. A family that might never see her the way she needed. He wanted to rage against the injustice of it. He wanted to howl at the fact that, for the first time in his life, there was nothing he could do about it.

You're wrong. This isn't the first time.

Memories sucker punched him in the gut. His mother walking away, without even looking back, her last words to him written on his soul.

No! He would not let that happen. Not again. He would show Marit that she had a choice. That she could have the future she wanted away from Svardia, away from duty and people who were blind to just how incredible she was. She could have a future *with him*, if she would just take it and let the rest burn. Kozlov, the shares, the whole damn lot.

Determination filled his thoughts and actions as he launched out of bed, putting his quick mind to work on a plan that would not only fulfil the last item on her list still left to complete, but also show her that she had a choice.

Marit looked at the blindfold with a great deal of suspicion. Not because she didn't trust Lykos, but because she knew that her scepticism made it fun. And she wanted the rest of their time together to be that. Fun.

Last night Marit had come back from her shower to find Lykos deeply asleep. Yes, she'd missed his touch, the feel of him within her, the memory so powerful it made her ache with need but, knowing how difficult he found it, she couldn't begrudge him the rest. Instead, she'd used the time to just take him in. To learn the rhythm of his breath, the pulse of his heartbeat, the pitch of the sigh that sometimes

escaped his lips. She'd spent half the night just looking at him. Imprinting everything she would need
to take with her.

'Marit?'

'A blindfold?'

'We have one last thing to tick off your list. And
this is the only way to do it properly.'

Tomorrow they would have to return to Svardia,
but today he was making sure she had done everything she had wanted to do before she became the
royal replacement for her sister. She reached for the
blindfold in his hands, pulling him into a kiss she
poured everything into.

Lykos groaned. '*Agápi mou*, if you do that we'll
never leave the bedroom.'

'Would that be so terrible?'

'No. But, despite my very healthy and totally war-
ranted ego, I promise you this will be better.'

Marit let out a shocked cry of indignation. 'Surely
not! Wash your mouth out,' she replied, making him
laugh and chasing away the last of the shadows in
his eyes. He circled her then, capturing her within
his embrace, and gently placed the blindfold over
her eyes.

'Yes?' he asked before covering them completely.
She placed her hand over his, bringing the blindfold
against her eyes.

'Yes,' she replied, handing him her complete trust.

Marit could smell the sea and hear the thrust of the
waves against…not sand, not a beach, but against a

barrier. They must be in a port. As if in confirmation, she heard the deep bass of a ship's horn burst beneath shouted voices and gulls crying overhead. She smiled, the inkling of where Lykos was taking her growing by the second.

After a conversation between Lykos and someone, he led them forward, warning her to watch her step. She wobbled a little in his hold as the ground beneath her changed to what must have been a short platform and she was led carefully down some steps at the other end into what she knew was a boat by the way it swayed beneath her.

'Can I take the blindfold off now?' she asked with a smile so wide she couldn't contain it.

'Not yet, *agapoúla mou*. Your list was very clear. Twenty-four hours out of sight and contact with the world.'

You are my world. The thought threatened to rob her of her smile, of her joy, but she wouldn't let it. There would be time to mourn the loss of what she would never have, but not yet. She wouldn't waste their time like that. Instead, she nodded and allowed Lykos to lead her to a cushioned seat as a few more shouted exchanges were made and finally the boat beneath her was set free.

That was how it felt as the boat launched forward. As if once unleashed the boat danced on the water. There was something so musical about the way it swayed from one side to another. Still blindfolded, she held the edge of the seat, bracing herself against the rise and fall of the boat against the waves. She squealed in delight like a child on a rollercoaster when she was hit with the sea salt spray and, encouraged by the sound of Lykos's laughter, she screamed again, *sure* that he steered them against the edge of the oncoming waves just for her.

Eventually the water became smoother and Lykos tried to remove the blindfold. But she shook her head. Here, in the darkness, there was no light on the sands of time that slipped through her fingers, there was no sun to illuminate the short steps left on their path.

The boat's motor cut out and they drifted gently. Lykos's steps towards her raised an expectation beneath her skin, wanting his touch, reaching out for it. She sensed him kneel before her, felt him take her hands in his own.

'If you keep it on, you won't see what I can see, and it is truly beautiful.'

He cupped her cheek and she leaned into what had become her most favourite place in the entire world. She didn't doubt what he'd said, she imagined the view was nothing short of spectacular, but right there, leaning into his palm was better than hearing her favourite song.

'The sea is sparkling, Marit. Like silk strewn with diamonds being shaken by the gods.' His words were a feast for her senses and she was helpless to resist. She slipped the blindfold from her eyes and took in a sight that was everything he'd described and more. She stood, Lykos rising with her, and she turned in full circle, seeing nothing and no one other than nature's beauty and Lykos.

Twenty-four hours out of sight and contact from the world.

She had written it as an impossible task. Something inconceivable. She should have known that this man, *only* this man, could have made it come true. He came to stand behind her, encircling her with his arms.

They were on a yacht. Not massive or obscenely ostentatious but perfect for two people. The sail was down, but she imagined that it would be a slice of brilliant white against the soft blue sky when raised. Wood the colour of butter lined the small vessel, every detail simple but exquisite. Silver lines gleamed in the sunlight and myriad shades of blue surrounded them as far as she could see. No land, no people, nothing but them.

'This is... Lykos, it's more than I could ever have imagined.'

There was a pause. 'I know what you mean.'

Suddenly they were talking about something else. Something that she simply couldn't face.

'Marit—'

She turned and pressed a kiss against his lips, stopping the words she couldn't bear to hear. Her hands plunged into his hair, holding him to her when he would have pulled away. He let the kiss linger as long as she needed it, but the man was more stubborn than she had given him credit for. He held her in his arms, offering her the world she'd always wanted and now could never have.

'Don't do it,' he said. 'I'll give you whatever you

need, take you wherever you want to go. I'll complete any list of things you like.'

Her eyes began to fill with tears she wouldn't dishonour him by wiping away.

'We'll run away. I'll find the most beautiful home for us and you'll fill it with music every day. You'll sing every day. We'll dance every day. And I'll—'

'Lykos, don't,' she said, shaking her head to stop his words. She couldn't trust herself not to give into what he was saying, what he was offering, because it was everything her heart wanted. And then she saw it. His jaw clenched and his eyes darkened the moment he felt her response as a rejection of him. 'No, Lykos—'

He turned from her and the pain she felt as he began to shut her out was devastating. 'Would I have ever been enough?' he asked, his gaze on the sea, pain glittering in his silvery eyes stealing the breath from her lungs.

'How could you ask that?'

'Are you going to tell me that the fact I grew up a child thief in an orphanage has nothing to do with why you won't be with me?'

'Lykos!' His words sliced little cuts into her heart, but she recognised them for what they were. A lifetime of hurt and rejection. 'Look at me,' she demanded, so he could see what was in her eyes, her heart. She waited and only when he turned towards her could she answer him. 'Everything you have done, everywhere you have been, it is a part of what makes you *you*. You shouldn't deny your past because it is the very thing that has driven you to achieve such incredible things. It's what makes you see the people most are blind to, makes you so generous with your time to those who deserve it, and what makes your heart so, so valuable, and you so amazing to me.'

It killed her to see the distrust in his eyes.

'Then tell me, if the legislation wasn't in place, would you marry me?'

Her heart stuttered at his question, stumbling over the thought that he might have wanted to marry her and the realisation that even then she couldn't. She felt tears gathering in her eyes, and he must have seen it because darkness swept into his eyes and she hated herself but she could never lie to him.

'No.'

'But you would have married André? And it's *not* because of where I came from?' His question was loud, angry and full of hurt and disbelief.

'No.'

'Then what is it?' he demanded.

'*Me!*' she couldn't help but yell back. 'It's me! I've changed, Lykos. Because when I ran away to marry André I was only thinking of myself. I was ignoring the fact that Aleksander didn't *want* me to make an advantageous marriage, he *needed* me to. The second in line to the throne must marry someone titled for the sake and security of the royal family and our country. Marrying André—marrying you—would be so selfish,' she said, shaking her head, her heart breaking over what she wanted with every fibre of her being, what she couldn't have. 'But if I am going to do this properly then I have to do it all, including marrying someone with a title.'

Lykos glared at her. 'And this has nothing to do with you trying to prove yourself worthy to a family that has never seen you, loved you, for who you truly are?' he accused.

It hurt how closely his question cut to the bone. She couldn't deny that there was a truth there, but it wasn't the sole reason behind her decision. In the last few days she had changed so much and it was because of Lykos. She had flourished in the freedom he had given her and, in that, found herself—even if it had cost her her heart.

'Tell me you don't love me,' he demanded, not waiting for an answer to his earlier question.

Every part of her ached to say that she did, burned to tell him how much she loved him. But she couldn't. 'Please,' she begged, 'don't make me another person in your life who tells you they love you before leaving you.'

He closed his eyes, his inhalation sharp and swift, speaking only of pain, the muscle flexing at his jaw, and her heart ached for him, for her, and for what they would never have.

'They don't deserve you.' Lykos's reply came strong and true, a slash of his hand through the air.

She cast her gaze to the floor, unable to stand the ferocity and truth in his gaze. 'That may be. But Svardia does.'

She looked up, letting him see how much this

cost her, let it shine from her eyes. She poured out
her hurt into the seascape and let the salt tears flow.
Her sob caught in her chest and the first, 'Sorry,'
came whispered on her breath, then another, then
another, until all around them her apologies echoed
until Lykos swept her into his arms and soothed the
deep sorrow lying in her heart.

He brushed her hair from her damp face and
pressed kisses to her heated skin, her forehead, her
cheeks, beneath her ear, her lips, her lips again, and
slowly her mouth opened to his, wanting him selfishly just one last time. She came to life beneath his
touch, her hands reaching for the front of his shirt,
fisting the cotton, the buttons straining. She feared
that she wanted so much it would never be satiated.
Until a want deeper, more primal rose within her.
One that was urgent and hot and just as desperate,
but the exact opposite. Now she needed to give.

Lykos felt the change in her ripple beneath her skin
and taste different on her tongue. It felt like…power.
She pulled him into a kiss that forced the sea to move
differently beneath his feet, as if they were pushing
against an impossible tide and for just this moment
in time they might succeed.

Arousal swept him up in a storm, ignited by the
passion twisting and unfolding in his arms, burning
through the ache in his heart. There would be time
to feel it later, long after he had returned Marit to
Svardia. But he could not, *would* not, damage her by
removing her from what she felt was her place in the
world. He'd felt the strength of her decision, the way

that it had settled about her shoulders. It wasn't because she felt she *had* to; it was what she needed to
do for her sister, her family and her country.

He pulled back from her kiss, her hair a wild halo
of gold, picking up the flecks of yellow starbursts in
her eyes that looked like the feathers of a phoenix.
Her lips were kiss-bruised, a flush riding high on
her cheeks, her breath as ragged as his own. If this
was their last day together then he would make sure
that it was spectacular.

He lifted her in his arms, the squeak of surprise
drawing a curve to his determined lips, delight un-
furling within him as her legs instinctively wrapped
around his waist and hooking at the ankles behind
him. Finally, her lips were level with his and he took
full advantage. He plundered her mouth for treasure,
his tongue dancing with hers, teasing her, filling
her, foretelling exactly what he wanted to do with
her. She met him stroke for stroke, touch for touch,
but when she pressed herself against his arousal he
forced his grip to soften when everything in him
wanted to hold tighter, to draw her to him and never
let her go. But, like the phoenix she reminded him of
so much, he would *have* to let her go. She had risen,
changed, become the woman she was always meant
to be, so tomorrow she would fly.

The thought momentarily rocked him, until she
placed the softest of bites on his bottom lip. Arousal
flared within him and he took her mouth in a kiss
that was a sensual punishment for them both. She
gasped into his mouth and it went straight to his
erection, hardening him to near pain. Need became

an almost feral thing, and he palmed the underside of her thighs, bringing her even closer against his body. The suite below deck felt as if it were miles away, but she deserved more than the rough comfort of cushions on wood.

As if sensing the internal debate within him, 'Here,' she pronounced and shifted in his hold, sliding luxuriously down the length of his body and tearing at his shirt, uncaring of the buttons that went flying across the deck. Her hands were hot and fast against his skin and just as desperate as his own that pulled at her top, drawing it swiftly over her head. Impatient, he flicked the clasp of her bra, drawing the straps from her shoulders and throwing it aside. Nipples pebbled, he palmed her breasts, drawing cries of pleasure from Marit. Pressing into his touch, her head fell back, exposing the long length of her neck to his open-mouth kisses. He luxuriated in the taste of her skin, traces of salt from the earlier sea spray, urging him on, the flicker of her pulse against his tongue driving him wild.

She pulled at his hips, her fingers finding the fastening on his trousers, his hands reaching for the same on hers. Frantically they pulled and pushed at clothes, laughing in their desperation until they were naked beneath the soft blue sky, the sun's rays on their skin nothing compared to the heat that drew them together in a kiss so passionate, so powerful Lykos was branded to the depths of his very soul. She had imprinted herself on him and he would never be the same again. He knew it then as deeply as he knew that he loved her. When she left she would take a part of his soul with her and he would never be whole again. The thought curled within him, folding in on itself, and he tucked it away, knowing he could never reveal that to her, knowing that to do so would cause her even more harm.

So, instead, he touched her, covering her with his palms, learning every single inch of her body, her chest, the swell of her abdomen, the dip of her hip and the curve of her backside, her skin hot and smooth and, between her legs, wet with need that only he could sate.

Lykos dropped to his knees before her, gently parting her legs and folds and, before she could say anything, swept his tongue across her clitoris, drawing a pleasure from her so pure she would have fallen had he not been holding her in place against his mouth.

The decadence of it stole her breath. Naked to the world, being pleasured by a man who knelt at her feet. He made her feel like a queen. The sweep of his tongue had her trembling, hot and needy. She felt both powerful and utterly weak at the same time as he hurled her towards an orgasm that nearly scared her with its intensity. One palm on the curve of her ass, the other on the inside of her thigh, she felt possessed, owned and branded by him.

She felt every single sweep of his tongue, every single full-blooded heartbeat pulsing through her veins, every single spark that exploded in her heart. She luxuriated in an arousal that became something almost threateningly powerful, but it was a power she wielded. It was as if she were at the bow of a

great ship, hurtling into mountainous waves knowing they could not hurt her. Knowing that she was
protected by him and his love. As if that knowledge,
that awareness, was all she had needed to push her
over the edge of her orgasm, Marit shattered into
a thousand pieces, assured that Lykos would catch
every single one of them and hold her together until
she could do it for herself.

When Marit came back to herself she was lying
against the breadth of Lykos's chest, anchored by
his legs and gazing lazily over the yacht's rails, his
hands brushing over her arms. His chin was resting
against the top of her head and she wanted so much
to stay there it hurt.

They were on the cushioned seat and there were
plates of delicious-looking food and a metal bucket
containing a bottle of champagne dripping cool con-
densation onto the wooden deck beside them.

There were so many things she wanted to say in
that moment. That she was sorry she couldn't be the
person he deserved, he *needed*. That she would be
yet another person to walk away from his love—it
hurt her, changed her on a fundamental level. There
were many ways that Lykos had impacted on who
she was, but this was the most devastating.

She couldn't imagine him walking through life
alone. She wanted more for him even if she couldn't
have it for herself.

'So, who will you kidnap next?' she asked, forcing
herself to have a conversation that made her stomach
burn and her tongue ache.

He stilled beneath her, his fingers halfway be-

tween her shoulder and elbow, and she forced her
body to relax, instead summoning the teasing tone
she'd once relished so much between them. She
twisted and looked up at him, having to shade her
eyes from the sun, but his eyes burned just as bright
and fierce and she steeled herself.

'That is not funny, *ángele mou.*'

'I know,' she said sadly, apology in her eyes.
'But—'

'Stop.'

'Lykos—'

'No. Marit, you made your decision. I cannot
stand it, but I *understand* it and I respect it. You
should do the same.'

Marit felt the sob rising in her chest, but she
couldn't. She couldn't cry any more. They didn't
have enough time.

'You deserve love, Lykos.'

'So do you.' His words were harsh, almost a bark.
To anyone else they would be accusatory. To her, they
were a stubborn declaration that his future was her
future, even if they weren't together.

She climbed up his body, her lips needing his,
her heart needing his touch and his love, even if
just for these last few hours. As the sun rose and
fell over the Aegean, the yacht swaying as gently
as possible on the rise and fall of the waves, they
talked, soothed, ate, drank and made love again and
again until a dawn so beautiful it was talked about
across the whole of Greece rose over the sea, herald-
ing Marit's return to Svardia.

CHAPTER ELEVEN

THE JOURNEY FROM Greece to Svardia on Lykos's private jet was too short, as if time had sped up as the last grains of sand slipped through Marit's fingers. The wide arc of the sky as the small plane banked to land was as familiar to Marit as the turn in the winding drive leading to the palace front door, but it still felt strange. As if it was happening to someone else—a dream—and that her time in Europe had been the reality.

How, she wondered, was it possible that she had only been gone for five days? It felt more like five years. She twisted her hands in her lap, a nervous gesture she hadn't performed since Lykos had swept her up on the morning of her supposed wedding, thrown her over his shoulder and walked out of the hotel with her.

Looking back on it, it was a miracle that there had been no press to witness it. But, thinking it through logically, knowing Lykos the way she did now, she wouldn't have put it past him to make sure they were otherwise occupied at that exact moment. The cabin

crew member announced their imminent arrival and
Marit looked away, not seeing the beautiful sculp-
tured gardens of the palace, the maze where she had
once got lost, the large trees she had hidden in as a
child.

Instead, she saw the sun glinting off a rippling
sea, she felt the heat of its rays on her skin, turning
it pink through the day and slightly bronze as the sun
set. She'd caught her reflection in the plane's bathroom mirror and wondered how it was that she appeared to look so healthy just as her heart shattered
into a million pieces.

She'd not been able to look at Lykos the entire
flight. She'd felt his gaze occasionally on her, but
he'd not tried to break her silence, as if he'd known
she needed it. Because if she opened her mouth, how
could she *not* tell him to turn the plane around? Beg
him to take her back to his yacht. To give her one
more day, week, month, year. To give her for ever.

She'd meant what she'd said to him on the yacht.
And even in the bar in the hotel in Milan. She would
have always come back. And yes, there was a part of
her that feared—as Lykos had accused—that she was
trying too hard to prove herself, to her parents, to her
siblings, to *herself* even, by doing what her family
and country needed her to do. But for her sister, to
whom she owed so much, her brother, who would
be an excellent king, and her people, who were kind
and generous, proud and determined… She could
never let them down the way her parents had let her

down. They deserved this from her and she would do it with all the broken pieces of her heart.

When the plane drew to a stop on the private runway in the palace grounds she released the safety belt, stood and smoothed out the crinkles in her trousers and swallowed a sad laugh before it got to her lips. The wrinkles were hardly going to be a surprise to anyone. She steeled herself. It would take time to overcome her reputation as the most disastrous princess in Europe. But she would.

She took a moment as Lykos talked to the crew unfolding the stairs onto Svardian soil. This was it. When she put her foot onto palace grounds it would be done. The decision irrevocable. She would be going straight to the office of her brother, the King. A timeline for the press announcement about Freya giving up her title and Marit becoming second in the line of succession to the throne would be decided. And if she knew her brother at all he would want her engaged to someone appropriate by the time the announcement was made.

Someone appropriate.

The phrase burned her throat as if the words dripped acid on her soul. Lykos was so much more than *appropriate* and she hated that she had made him feel less than that. But this was the moment she had to make peace with it. She would take the love she had for him, the love she had felt from him and make that enough. She breathed in deeply, hearing the tremble and mewl of the *rebetiko* music from the

Greek tavern crying for her and Lykos and ached for a
future she was actively choosing to walk away from.

Finally, this time when she felt his gaze on hers,
she met it head-on, nodding once determinedly in
that way she had borrowed from him. Her heart
turned viciously as she walked up the narrow plane
aisle and she passed him to take the steps down onto
the tarmac to return to the palace.

Lykos waited in the corridor outside Aleksander's
office, as far from Marit as he could be. She had
slowly been distancing herself from him since they'd
returned the yacht and boarded the plane. He'd felt
it deep down and hated every second of it. But he
wouldn't dishonour her or himself by asking her
again. She'd told him that first day, when they were
in Milan.

I will always go back.

She'd never once lied to him. But why did it feel
so very much as if they were lying to themselves?

He cast a gaze at the garish baroque style that
filled the entire Rilderdal Palace, everything in him
revolting at the symbols of money, snobbery, emo-
tional neglect and manipulation that it had all come
to mean to him since knowing Marit.

Princess Marit.

He shook his head. The last person he'd thought
he'd ever fall for. There she was on the other side of
a hallway, less than two metres away, but as far from
his reach as the moon. He clenched his jaw, straining
at the reins that held him back: his promise to her to

respect her decision. A door behind them creaked open and a small, plain-faced brunette caught Marit's eye with a sympathetic smile.

'Henna,' Marit said, meeting the woman with a warm embrace. 'Have you heard from Freya?' she asked, pulling back. 'I've been trying to reach her.'

'She's okay,' Henna replied. 'She's just out of contact at the moment.' When the dark-haired woman cast a glance in his direction he wondered how on earth Marit had failed to see the other woman's evasion. Then again, Marit only had thought for what lay beyond the door to her brother's office. The brunette nodded to him in deference and Lykos resisted the urge to laugh. If he hadn't, the sound would have been bitter and cynical and, once again, his soul lashed out at the self-imposed restraints.

'He will see you both now,' Henna announced, finally drawing Marit's gaze to his. Both as confused as the other, they passed Henna, who held the door open to them and closed it, leaving them alone with King Aleksander of Svardia.

He was leaning back against the front of his desk, flicking through a manila folder that seemed to contain more than a few pages. He might have appeared distracted, but Lykos knew how devious Aleksander could be when he wanted—or didn't want—something. Refusing to make eye contact with his audience was definitely a power play by the King.

But Lykos was done with games and he had nothing left to lose. The shares he'd wanted to bring Kozlov down had completely lost all meaning. Let someone else deal with the bastard. Lykos was here for one reason only. To make sure that Marit was returned safely. After that? The only thing Lykos saw in his future was alcohol. A lot of it.

'Still unmarried?' It was the first thing that Aleksander said to his little sister after she'd run halfway around Europe just to find some kind of independence from this family, and it cut Lykos to realise just how little Aleksander knew his sister. *Saw* her.

'Yes, Your Majesty. I am still unwed.'

Aleksander narrowed his eyes as if something in her response didn't suit.

Lykos fisted his hands behind his back, but Aleksander's gaze briefly landed on him as if he'd seen the motion, before returning to Marit.

'And you are ready to take Freya's position within the family. Her duties and…her *obligations*.'

It was an outrage to hear him talk of marrying off his sister as a family duty or obligation. Lykos would have dragged her with him into the greatest of poverties knowing that her love was more valuable than any position, any status, any amount of money.

'Yes.'

There was nothing but pure conviction in the woman standing beside him. She was completely still even though she was taking a sledgehammer to what remained of his heart. He couldn't bear to stand here and watch this. But he would. For her. Because somehow he knew that while she couldn't look at him, couldn't touch him, she needed him here for this.

'André will keep his mouth shut?'

'Yes.' Lykos surprised the siblings by answering this time. He would make absolutely sure that nothing would taint Marit ever again.

Aleksander nodded in acknowledgement. 'I must say, Marit, even I hadn't thought of that loophole. I'm impressed. Marrying *before* you ascend to second in line to the throne could have really opened up the playing field.'

Lykos almost choked at her brother's tone. He knew Aleksander to be a lot of things, but this seemed particularly cruel.

'But never mind,' the King pressed on, 'I have found the perfect candidate to be your consort.'

'Yes, Your Majesty.'

Lykos raged in silence. Had she so little care about herself now that she didn't even want to know? To ask who it was her brother had found for her to marry? To have *children* with?

'But we are on a very short timeline, so the wedding will have to take place in three days' time. I am aware that this is *difficult*—'

This time Lykos actually scoffed. Out loud. This was her family? This was her future?

'But we have very few options available to us.'

'Of course. If I may be excused? There are things I need to attend to before the announcement.'

It was as if he weren't even there. As if he were being forced to watch this travesty take place and was utterly powerless and helpless to stop it because she'd asked him not to.

'If you mean your youth orchestra, then I've taken care of it.'

It was the only time during this farcical encounter that Marit showed any sign of reaction. She was shocked, Lykos could see, but she reined it in immediately.

'It will be included in your duties as second in line to the throne.'

'Thank you, Your Majesty. I would still like to speak to them personally about the change in my status if that is okay.'

There was a tic throbbing in Aleksander's jaw as if she had angered him somehow, not that Marit could have seen it as her eyes were cast somewhere over her brother's shoulder.

'Yes, you may leave.'

There was a moment, the space of a heartbeat when he thought that she might look at him, that she might meet his gaze for one last time. Her lips trembled for just a second, until she bit down on the bottom one as if to hold it in place, and turned away from him, from her brother, and left the room.

The moment she left he glared at Aleksander. 'You would do that to your own sister?' he demanded.

'Are you going to stop me?'

For a moment it sounded like a genuine question, before Lykos realised that it could only be the arrogance of a king.

'She asked me not to,' he growled, even though everything in him wanted to do exactly that. To stop the man.

Aleksander shrugged his shoulder and walked around the desk to resume his seat behind it. Lykos's gaze fell on the folder left open on the desk. A full colour photograph and the name of the man Marit would marry.

'I will have my lawyers draw up the papers for the transfer of shares. I've always hated having them. I detest that man.'

Lykos forced a nod, not trusting himself to speak and unable to take his burning gaze from the photograph, his eyes quickly taking in the man's title: Prince Henrik. Lykos didn't bother with where he was from, the kid looked young. And weak. He might have a title, he might be a prince and fit for Aleksander's purpose, but he was *not* right for Marit.

'If there is nothing else?' the King asked.

In the silence between them Aleksander levelled him with a glare that screamed disappointment and disapproval, but Lykos was too angry to care. He turned on his heel and stalked from the room. He slammed the door behind him, not caring that the sound crashed through the palace. Fury rose so swift, so harsh, so *much*, it erupted. Spinning, Lykos slammed his fist into the palace wall, denting the plaster and damaging his knuckles, and still it didn't help. Nothing would help. Not now.

Marit sank beneath the layers of quilts and throws on her bed and still it did nothing to ward off the cold that settled in shivers across her shoulders. Her body trembled as if in shock, even though she told herself over and over again that she was doing the right thing. In three days' time she would be married. It didn't matter to whom. It wouldn't be Lykos and that was all that did matter. And as lonely and sad as the thought made her, it was Lykos her heart ached for.

She wanted her sister. She needed Freya to tell her that she was making the right choice. But she couldn't. If Freya knew what this was costing her, she wouldn't let her do it. Her sister had the biggest heart of anyone she knew and, no matter the consequences to herself, Freya would revoke her decision in a heartbeat. But it was time for Marit to become the Princess no one had ever expected her to be.

She reached for her phone and pressed the call icon beside her sister's name, knowing that, wherever she was, she wouldn't get the message probably until after Marit was married. She choked back the teary laugh that bubbled as she realised that, again, her sister wouldn't be there on her wedding day.

Please leave a message after the tone.

'Hi, Freya, it's me. I… I'm sorry that I ran. I'm sorry if you were worried. To be honest, I'm not sure where you are. Maybe *you're* running.' The thought made Marit smile a little. 'Should I be worried?' she half teased. Marit inhaled deeply. 'Thank you. I don't think I've ever really said that before. But thank you for being everything I needed growing up.' As Marit said the words she hadn't meant to, she realised how right they were. At every hurt, every pain she remembered, from excruciating dinner times, to night terrors, to hospital visits, Freya had been there. And, somewhere in the background, even Aleksander. It felt as if she had been searching for something her entire life that she would never get, and all along what she'd wanted had been right there in front of her.

'I know that I haven't been the easiest sister and that you've probably wanted to throttle me more times than not. And while things with Mama and Papa were difficult, you…you always made me feel loved. I might not have realised it at the time, but I do now. I have…' She broke off, trying to find the words. 'I *know* that now, the feeling of being loved. I know that, no matter what happens now or in the future, I will always have that. I didn't realise how rare that was, how much safety that love gave.'

Her voice broke on the last word, because it was absolutely the truth. She had been *seen* by him. *Loved* by him. And that had become an anchor for her. It had anchored her self-worth and sense of self and it was so strong and so deep that it had given her the strength she needed to do this.

'Please know that I do this because I want to. I do not and will never resent or place blame for the change in our succession. But I so wish you could be there. I'm not sure if you will get this in time, but my wedding day is in three days. And…if you can, I'd like that. Love you,' she finished quickly before the tears fell.

The next thing she did was pull up her messages, finding the name that she'd put into her phone back in Greece on the day of Theron and Summer's party.

She typed out a message in English.

Summer, please tell Theron that Lykos needs him urgently. This isn't a tease or payback. Please, just tell him?

Marit signed her name, hit send and then deleted Lykos's number from her contacts, deleted the sent messages to Summer and turned off her phone. The temptation to know how Lykos was would be too much for her. This was the only way that she could bear to go ahead with whatever marriage her brother had planned. Knowing that it was for the good of her family, her country...it was all that mattered.

Deep in the centre of the palace, Aleksander paced his room. Back and forth, back and forth. Things had not come about how he'd hoped. It infuriated him beyond belief, but it was not a decision he could make for them. Both Freya and Marit deserved so much more, which was why he'd put the plan into place in the first instance.

He stared out of the window, hoping that there was enough time for them to come to their senses. There was a knock on the door. He had needed to take his sister's lady-in-waiting into his confidence, not something he had enjoyed or wanted, but necessity had forced his hand. There were two people in the world he could trust and one of those was himself.

'They are waiting, Your Majesty.'

Aleksander nodded. 'Make the call.'

Henna's eyes flashed curiously, as if she wanted to admonish him. The thought was almost laughable. No one had dared try that for years. He simply stared at her until she managed to get herself under control. It took a remarkable amount of time to do, but he was a patient man and, besides, it gave him time to remember a little more about her family. And an idea seeded in his mind at that moment.

Just as she turned to go, he called her back. 'You have a sister, that is correct?' he asked, vaguely noticing the way her cheeks flushed. Curious.

'Yes, Your Majesty.'

'Single?'

'Yes, Your Majesty.'

'Your mother, she is a marchioness, is she not?'

This time her teeth clenched. Interesting. 'Yes, Your Majesty.'

'And your sister—?'

'Will inherit the title. Yes, Your Majesty.'

He raised a disapproving eyebrow and she responded in kind. *Fascinating.*

'I believe we are done here,' she stated.

'For now,' he warned, and she disappeared through the door.

CHAPTER TWELVE

LYKOS HAD REALISED the truth the moment he'd lain on his bed, staring out of the window at the moon rising over Paris, and in its silvery rays he'd seen Marit, her hair dancing on a breeze that he couldn't feel. She was the reason he'd been able to sleep. With her beside him, he'd not woken once and it had been the one and only time in his life he could remember that happening.

He'd not wanted to leave Svardia—to leave Marit—but he hadn't trusted himself to stay. So instead he'd come back to where it had all started. And he'd been confronted with Marit's wedding dress still crumpled in the middle of the living room floor as if she'd just stepped out of it.

He left it there, ignored it as he stripped off his clothes and took the longest shower he'd ever had, in the hope of washing whatever *this* was off him. Not even the dirt of the Athens streets had been so ingrained in his skin, in his psyche.

He let the water stream down around him until the

tank ran cold and still he stayed beneath the spray, beating against his skin until it was numb.

But if you're numb, why does it still hurt?

It was a facile question to ask himself, when he knew the answer well enough.

Because I love her. I will always love her.

With that thought he slammed off the water, jerked back the shower door, leaving it rattling, and stalked into his room.

'*Theé mou*, Lykos, do you always walk around naked?'

'Only when there are unexpected guests,' Lykos replied without even looking up. Without even caring that Theron was there in his apartment. He couldn't even raise the energy to be shocked or surprised. 'I'll turn around if it will spare your blushes,' he threw over his shoulder as he reached the wardrobe and grabbed a pair of loose linen trousers and a long-sleeved white tee.

'Well, that's hardly better,' Theron said, standing in the bedroom doorway with his hands on his hips, his jacket flaring slightly behind the bracket of his arms. 'Now you look like some male catalogue model,' he accused, flicking his hand up and down.

Lykos simply glared at the man who was as close to him as a brother and left the room, forcing Theron to turn to make space for him to do so.

'How did you get in?' Lykos asked, mildly curious, as he walked barefoot to his alcohol cabinet, picked a glass and poured an unhealthy amount of whisky into it.

'I'm the head of an internationally renowned and respected security firm, Lykos. It would be worrying if I *couldn't* get in.'

Lykos paused for a beat, nodded in agreement and thew back the measure of whisky in the glass and poured himself another.

'Do I get one, or are you planning to drink the whole bottle yourself?'

'I was absolutely planning to drink the whole bottle myself and consider it an act of rudeness that you didn't bring your own,' Lykos declared as he ignored the wedding dress in the living area that Theron was staring suspiciously at and pulled back the French window to access the balcony.

He padded out onto the wooden decking, placed his glass on a chair and set about building the logs and firelighters in the firepit, wondering if he could put the dress on it in one go, or whether he'd have to cut it up. Suddenly the image of him sitting there with a pair of scissors, cutting a wedding dress into strips and feeding it into a fire seemed a little overly dramatic and he decided that he'd wait until Theron was gone.

The door slid open a little wider and Theron stepped out onto the decking and went to stand at the balcony, looking over the Paris skyline.

'Nice digs,' he commented.

Lykos barely spared him a grunt. Finally, he struck the match and threw it into the bottom of the triangle he'd built and stood back, watching the flames catch and twist and wished he hadn't because he instantly thought of Marit.

'Are you okay, Lykos?'

'Don't be such a girl. Of course I'm okay,' he growled.

'Liar.'

Lykos wasn't sure whether it was Theron's voice he heard, or Marit's.

'Honestly, after the crap you pulled with me and Summer, you think you're going to get out of this so easy? No chance.' Theron placed a bottle of whisky that had most definitely *not* been in his alcohol cabinet on the side table and took a seat as if he was moving into the apartment.

'What do you want from me?' Lykos demanded.

'First I'd like to know why you're even here and not in Svardia getting your woman back.'

'Promise me never to say that again. You sound like some eighties neanderthal. She's *not* my woman, she's a goddamn princess and you will treat her with the respect she deserves.'

'Okay!' Theron said, raising his hands in surrender, the glass of whisky wedged between his little finger and thumb. But the tease in his tone didn't last for long and eventually Theron levelled him with a gaze that Lykos knew was very close to the line. He wouldn't accept anything but the truth now.

'Everything I've done, everything I've achieved, earned, worked for. Everything I have. It was all for nothing.'

'What on earth are you talking about?' Theron demanded as if Lykos was mad.

'I wasn't enough for her.' Shame cut through Lykos as he said the words. He stared at the ground between his feet, hating that he felt so much hurt, so much agony. Hating that Marit in any way reminded him of his mother. Hating the way he wasn't sure which woman he was talking about. Hating that it made him tear up. 'She walked away without a backward glance.'

They both had.

He clenched his jaw, hoping that somehow it would stop the press of wet heat against his eyes, that it would force down the swell of agony rising in his chest as he fought a sense of rejection and abandonment so acute that, if he'd been standing he would have fallen. Even now he was half afraid he might not get back up. His breath shuddered silently, the crackle and pop of the fire, the distant sounds of the Aegean on the Piraeus shoreline filled the silence for what felt like an eternity and somehow Lykos had known what Theron would ask.

'Did you ever look for her? Your mother?'

'She told me not to. She told me it was for her own protection. That Aeolus would use me to hurt her and keep hurting her. Tell me, Theron,' Lykos demanded, glaring up at his old friend, 'how could I have looked for her? How could I have, knowing, believing truly, that it would cause her physical harm?'

Lykos's gut twisted, not feeling as sure as he had once done as a teenager.

'And after we found out he'd died? I don't get it. You kept track of Summer's mother for years…but not your own.'

The words sliced, quick and clean, at his heart. Lykos shook his head. 'I…' Shame and grief and loss swirled like a noxious substance in his stomach. 'What if she didn't want me? What if she'd moved on and I was a reminder of *him*? What if all I could ever be to her was pain?'

The empathy burning in Theron's eyes was almost enough to push him over the edge. He shook his head again. The friend closer to him than any brother could have been put a hand on his shoulder.

'Lykos, we all make mistakes. As children, when it is done by adults, it is inconceivable to us. Your mother thought what she was doing was right, of that I have no doubt. But if you want to find out, to track her down, then know that we'll be here for you. Summer, me. Even Kyros. You think you don't have a family, you think you're alone, but we're here. For you. So if you ever want to find her, say the word. It's done.'

Reeling with shock from Theron's words, his offer, Lykos realised that he'd never, not once, wondered if his mother had made the wrong decision. Perhaps because he'd had to be completely sure that she was right because emotionally that had been the only way he could make peace with the situation.

It was as if a giant fissure had cracked open in the ground beneath him.

'What?' demanded Theron, who must have picked up on it.

'My mother was trying to do the right thing.'

'Of course,' Theron replied as if it were obvious, and then, his eyes narrowing in understanding, 'like Marit,' he concluded.

But Lykos had to dispute it. 'Theron… She is a *princess*. I am little more than a street thief with a bank account.'

Theron was silent for a long time. Long enough to draw Lykos's gaze.

'Is that what you think? *Skatá*, Lykos. I saw the way she looked at you.'

'It doesn't matter.'

'Do you love her?'

'With every single beat of my heart and breath I have left on this earth.' The sincerity of his words spoke to the depth of their souls as if it were a prayer and a promise. For a shocking second Lykos felt a hot damp heat against his eyelids and fisted his hands until it went away. He used the anger. Fed off it to push the sorrow back down where it belonged. He wrestled with the idea that she might have made a mistake, thought through the logic and tested it against what he knew of her and her situation.

'She is sacrificing herself and they don't even see it. Her family, they are supposed to protect her. They are supposed to put her first. I swear, Theron, if she marries this guy, it will kill her. Slowly, bit by bit and day by day, it will ruin everything that is pure and perfect about her.'

Words choked in his throat and he threw back another mouthful of whisky to ease the tightness.

'You want me to dig up some dirt on him?' Theron offered.

'And, what, we blackmail them? They're kings, Theron. *Actual* royalty.'

'And maybe you're letting that mess with your head.'

'What do you mean?' Lykos growled in warning.

'You were the greatest pickpocket in Athens, Lykos, or are you so ashamed of your past that you forget who you were? Who you *are*,' he stressed, staring Lykos dead in the eye with a determination and fire that Lykos felt in his soul. 'You say that it will kill her, marrying this guy? Then stop it. Do what you have to do to save her. She might want to do what is right, Lykos, but if you say it's wrong I believe you and I will support you one hundred per cent.'

'And I do what, kidnap her on her wedding day, *again*?'

'For real this time? Absolutely. So, what do you say?'

'I say,' Lykos said, standing from the chair, 'that the Pickpocket of Piraeus is going to attempt his greatest act of thievery yet. I'm going to steal a princess.'

Marit stood in the stone corridor of the Svardian family chapel. It had been there for as long as there had been a palace. She smoothed a palm over the

large solid blocks of stone that made up the walls
of the small church. Cold to the touch, Marit found
it fitting somehow. Beyond dark wooden doors, her
brother, the priest and her groom waited. The agreement between the two families had been made, Marit
not really aware of the specifics. Her brother's mach-
inations had long since stopped surprising her. Her
greatest regret was simply that her sister wasn't there.

Her parents were still on their year-long sabbati-
cal, protocol thankfully meaning that they were out
of contact to all their children for the first three hundred and sixty-five days of the new monarch's rule.
Marit didn't mind so much about the parents who had
been little better than absent for most of her life, but
she missed Freya terribly.

She wasn't quite sure where Freya was. She could
have sworn that she'd heard one of the staff talk
about her return to the palace, but Marit hadn't been
able to find her and she wasn't answering her calls.
Her absence had stung at first, until she remembered
that her sister wasn't the source of her hurt and it had
lessened the ache in her chest. Instead, Marit had
drawn on the love she'd felt from Lykos to fill the
void in her heart, realising that in the end, whether
she spoke to Freya or not, she would marry Prince
Henrik and do her duty by her country.

She ran a slightly damp hand down the front of her
dress, smoothing imaginary wrinkles from the silk.
It was a pretty dress this time and, while it might
not be what she would have chosen for herself—an

image of the stunning dress she'd worn to Victoriana flashing in her mind's eye—at least it fitted.

Footsteps clacked on the stone flooring, coming towards her, and for an insane moment she hoped that it was Lykos, come to whisk her away. Her heart pounded in her chest and her cheeks flushed with anticipation, her hopes crashing to the ground when she caught sight of Henna coming around the corner.

'Your Highness?' she said, rushing towards Marit in concern.

'I'm…fine, thank you, Henna. I don't suppose you've seen Freya?'

Henna's eyes clouded and she shook her head, her lips a thin grim line.

Marit nodded, telling herself that it was okay. That it didn't hurt.

'Are you…sure that this is what you want?' Henna asked. 'You need to know that you have a choice here, Marit. You don't have to marry Henrik.'

Marit was taken by her tone—the sincerity and assurance in it was powerful and strong. But the thing was, she knew that she didn't have to. Yes, Marit wished things were different, but her sister was stepping down and her family and her country needed her. She dug deep within herself and found the strength she needed.

'It's okay. I'm ready.'

A simple piano version of Pachelbel's 'Canon in D' played as Marit took her first steps down the aisle. She wore a simple veil, short across her shoulders, falling lower at the back, and through the cream gauze the chapel took on an ethereal quality. Her brother stood behind a man who looked familiar only in that she had seen photographs of the Prince. He seemed…young. With each step she took in not the man she was to marry but the ways in which he wasn't Lykos. He wasn't dark-haired like Lykos, he wasn't as tall or broad as Lykos, his jaw wasn't as strong, his eyes didn't spark silver shards that she could stare at for hours.

She mentally shook herself, knowing that it was cruel to be comparing Henrik to a man he never had a hope of matching. This was different, Marit told herself. This would only ever be… Her footsteps faltered and her gaze flickered to her brother's. There was something there, something in Aleksander's eyes, that she hadn't seen before. Worry? Concern? Regret?

All thoughts, however, were wiped from her mind as the wooden doors behind her burst open and clattered furiously against the stone walls. Shock sliced through her, causing her—and everyone else in the chapel—to turn.

Framed in the now open doorway, Lykos looked like an avenging angel. He filled the space, sunlight streaming in behind him, casting him in shadow, and the lock of hair fallen across his forehead seemed almost purposely disrespectful somehow. Lykos cast a look over her shoulder, but Marit only had eyes for him and her heart soared, even as her mind blanked.

He stalked down the aisle, the first step apparently

enough to prompt the priest to ask what was going on. Marit half expected her brother to step forward, but he didn't. She knew that she should move, should stop Lykos, should step from his path, but the sheer determination simmering in his eyes had struck her still. He had but one intent, a single focus so sure, and she knew—*knew* that he would not be stopped.

Within a heartbeat he had closed the short distance she'd travelled up the aisle and had stepped indecently close. Their ragged breaths billowed the gossamer-thin veil between them. Her hungry gaze consumed the sight of him. Her heart was pounding so hard in her chest she was surprised it didn't echo around the small chapel like the whispers of the men behind her. She wanted to weep and sigh and reach for him and push him away all at once. She followed his gaze to where it had been caught, flickering between her eyes and her mouth, finally homing in on her lips as if he wanted nothing more than to feast upon them.

'Forgive me?'

His words were so unexpected it took her a moment to register them. 'For what?' she asked, just as a smile curved wickedly at his lips.

'For this,' he said. It was all the warning he gave her as he grasped her wrist, bent slightly, leaned into her and hauled her over his shoulder as he straightened.

'Lykos!' she screamed.

Her cry cut sacrilegiously through the serenity of the chapel, met by a chorus of shocked gasps from the groom and the priest.

* * *

Lykos shifted Marit on his shoulder, one hand securing her in place, the other pointing at Aleksander, his heart finally settling now that he had his hands on her. He angled himself towards a tableau he would have found amusing had it not been so tragic.

'This is done,' he announced to Aleksander. 'She will not be your puppet any more.'

Aleksander nodded. Lykos was surprised to see what could have been satisfaction in the King's eyes.

'She deserves your words, *Your Majesty*,' he growled. Marit needed to hear it. Needed to know that her family weren't using her and that they wouldn't come after her. There would be time for them to discuss it properly, but for now she had to know that she had a *true* choice. Only then would she be free.

'Yes. She can go now.'

A relief so vast and so sure swept through Lykos in an instant and he had to force his lungs to work as if for the very first time.

'And Kozlov?' the King demanded.

It wasn't even a contest. He would choose Marit. Every. Single. Time.

'He's your problem now. I'll transfer my shares to you so that you have the majority. I am sure you will find a suitable way to dispense with him.'

'I will,' the King confirmed, before raising a hand to stop Lykos from turning when he would have. 'She needed someone who would fight for her,' Aleksander said, his tone as much a warning as an explanation. In that moment, Lykos understood a different interpretation of events than how he had seen them only moments before.

He could only hope that Marit's brother deserved that interpretation.

'*Entáxei*, we are done,' Lykos announced as he stalked from the chapel, making his way past Henna. He was about to thank her, as he would not have been able to return to the palace without her help, but she waved him off before he could form the words, glancing back to the chapel where her King was watching her every move. Lykos would have wished her luck, but wondered whether Aleksander might need it more.

He walked out into the sunshine as male voices behind him were raised in what sounded like a nauseating outburst. Words like *outrageous*, *unbelievable*, *disrespectful* filled the air in a deeply whiney tone until a very commanding, 'Enough!' stopped the flow. Lykos was happy to leave Aleksander to it. The man had made his bed, he needed now to lie in it.

'Lykos—'

'Not yet,' he interrupted. He might have won the battle but not the war. He needed to focus on what came next, and he couldn't do that with his hand on the curve of Marit's backside, holding her to him and destroying concentration.

He approached his convertible and pressed the key fob so kindly replaced by the dealership. The locks clicked satisfyingly as he came to the passenger side door, pulled it open and poured her into it. There was less tulle this time, the affair much sleeker than it had been ten days ago, but he still wasn't happy with her dress. She looked, once again, as if she were playing dress-up, but this time it came off as old, staid, serious. All the things that she was *not*.

Marit fumed up at him from the seat of the car as he shut the door on her, but simmering beneath the glare was heat. Heat and something he didn't quite yet dare to hope for. Lykos rounded the car, half expecting her to flick the locks, but she didn't. He couldn't tell whether that was a good or bad sign.

He opened the door and slid behind the wheel, his hands wrapping around it to stop himself from reaching for her, from dragging her to him in a kiss that would never end. There were things that needed to be said.

'Lykos—'

'Not *yet*,' he said again, unsure that he could trust himself to say what he needed to if she distracted him. 'I need you to know that, no matter what, you can go. You can go anywhere. You don't have to choose me. You don't have to feel obliged or indebted. Your life is your own now. I know what you were doing. Aleksander and Freya know too. And clearly it meant a lot to them, for you to be willing to make a sacrifice of yourself.'

'Ly—'

He pinched the bridge of his nose and squinted his eyes shut. 'Marit, so help me, if you don't let me say this, I never will.' He practically felt the way her lips closed, imagining them pressed together between her teeth. 'The thing is,' he pressed on, 'they are your family. And they will support you, no matter what, just the way that you and Aleksander will support Freya. But you cannot expect them to see you, if you erase yourself in such a way. And I promise you, Marit. Marriage to that puffed-up Prince would have made you invisible.

'*Make* them see you by showing them who you are. By honouring yourself and them with choices that come from your heart,' he said, thumping his chest—which might have been a little dramatic but, dammit, that was how she made him feel. After all, he'd just kicked open the door of a church and walked off with a princess bride. 'And if that choice is not me, Marit, then,' he said, breath shuddering in his lungs, 'I will stand by that.'

The car was filled with silence for much longer than Lykos liked.

'Is that it?'

'What?' he asked, turning to face her.

'That's your big declaration, is it? Pick me? Choose me?'

'Well…yes,' he answered, a little stuck for words.

'I didn't hear anything about love in there. Not once,' she huffed—and his heart rose up in his throat at the sight of the tease in her eyes. Not that she wasn't right. He'd been so worried about making sure she knew that she didn't have to stay, he hadn't told her why she should.

'*Prinkípissa mou*, you are the key to my heart and everything that lies within it. It was closed, locked away until you snuck past defences that no one has *ever* breached. I might have been a criminal in my youth, but you are the real thief. You have stolen my heart for ever and I don't even want it back.

'Because I *see* you. The talented, crazy-hearted, beautiful, fiery, fun woman that you are. Because I see the incredible partner, the amazing wife and perfect mother you will be some day. And because I love you. With every single beat of my heart and breath in my lungs, I love you.'

Marit's eyes glistened, the shards of jade and gold glowing with a love that Lykos had to pinch himself to believe. Her lips had formed an O and a gentle sigh fell from them and warmed his heart.

'Lykos…'

He waited, but she remained silent. 'What is it?'

'Well, I had thought you might interrupt me, so I was giving you time.'

He glared at her, but it was such a mockery of anger, Marit knew that he enjoyed her tease as much as she did.

She reached for his hands, loosening their iron grip on the steering wheel and taking them in her own. She reached up to cup his jaw in her palm and her heart soared when he leaned into the affectionate touch.

'Thank you,' she said at first, because she did need to say it. 'I am sorry that I would have done you such a disservice in the name of duty.' He shook his head as if to ward off her apology. 'I…' She paused, finally allowing herself to believe that this was real.

That he had freed her from a duty she was *never* supposed to have borne. 'But what about Freya?'

'I believe that your brother has plans for her that will make things right.'

'Really?' Marit looked up, so very hopeful.

'Absolutely.'

With his confidence so assured, Marit's heart soared. 'I love you, Lykos. More than I ever thought possible. I didn't know that this was what it felt like, to be loved and to love. I didn't trust in it before but now I do,' she said, her heart trembling in her chest. 'You make me feel so special, so wanted and so loved, all I can hope to do is show you how much that means to me, each day for the rest of our lives.'

He turned the key in the ignition. 'We need to leave. Now.'

'What's the rush?'

'I need to get you out of that damn dress, because there's no way I'm proposing to you while you're wearing a wedding dress meant for another man,' he growled and floored the gas pedal. Her laughter pealed out of the open window as the Aston swept from the palace with a spray of gravel on the driveway as they began the first day of the rest of their lives together.

EPILOGUE

LYKOS SAT WITH his face turned to the sun, legs stretched out before him and his heart filled with love as he listened to the sounds of his children laughing and the delicate notes of the bouzouki being massacred. The high-pitched trill came to a sudden stop and a curse was uttered, low and angry.

'The children, Marit,' he called, eyes still closed, knowing that his voice would carry to her.

'That's Princess to you,' she yelled back grumpily.

He smiled as he heard a sigh, before the instrument was put down on the floor of the music room that led straight out onto the long garden, at the bottom of which ran a shallow stream the children adored. Her footsteps sounded closer and closer, her presence raising goosebumps across his skin even after ten years of marriage. He held his arm out to catch her as she passed, hands wrapping around her waist and hauling her into his lap, where his wife did a truly terrible job of trying to escape.

'You know I could run if I wanted to?' she said as his eyes finally opened to see her beauty.

'I know that you can do whatever you turn your heart to,' he said, knowing the words touched her by the way her eyes flared gold. 'Just perhaps not the bouzouki.'

She slapped at his arm and he pulled her closer and pressed kisses against her neck that went from playful to passionate the instant Marit groaned and shifted in his lap. He stilled, not because he didn't want to, but because the children would return soon, eagerly anticipating the arrival of Katy, Theron and Summer. Pressing his forehead to Marit's, he cupped her cheek and loved the way she leaned into his palm, appreciating how she instantly understood why he slowed his affection.

'*Agápi mou*, you just need patience.'

'It was never one of my strong points. But then you came along and then I learned—'

Marit's laughter burned bright as he went to kiss the tease from her lips and the passion that burned between them was still as bright as it had been when they had met. The day he'd kidnapped her for the second time, he had whisked her away on his private jet and flown them back to Paris, where he'd divested her of another wedding dress not meant for either of them and later, naked and satiated, he had proposed.

Of course, he'd then had to propose again properly and in the grandest way possible—in part because he'd discovered how Theron intended to surprise Summer and the drive to best him was irrefutable, but mainly because Marit deserved it. She deserved a man who would proclaim his love for her to the world. So each year he found new, devious, attention-grabbing ways to remind Marit that she was the most loved. He'd been doing rather well and even Theron was on the verge of admitting defeat, until Marit had bested them both with a gesture so grand and so impossible it was unbeatable.

As Marit gentled her kiss, she snuggled into his chest and they lay there in the sun, outstretched on a lounger until the sun passed behind the turret and they were momentarily cast in shade.

About a year after they'd married, Marit finally extracted why it was that Lykos had always wanted a castle. He'd never told a living soul, but it had started when his mother had told him stories while his father slept off his hangover. Stories of castles and maidens and an English thief called Robin Hood, the son of an Earl, who'd lost his lands and title when fighting in the Crusades and returned to England appalled by the poverty he'd found there. He'd robbed from the rich to give to the poor and Lykos had known that his mother had told him this story to make him feel better about doing his father's bidding. As a child, he'd decided that one day he would live in a castle and never have to steal another thing.

And his wish had come true. The last thing he'd stolen had been Marit's heart and he would never need anything again. Not even the castle Marit had made their home in. Lykos marvelled at how he felt more love now for Marit than he ever had. While she'd returned to university to study music and then later music therapy, he continued to work, but much less intensely. Marit had learned to play every instrument she could find and they had enough musical equipment to outfit an orchestra. Marit's youth project had been a roaring success even before Aleksander had kept his promise to support it.

His wife had an insatiable curiosity about almost everything and when she'd asked him to teach her how to steal wallets he'd laughed, but she'd been insistent. Aleksander still had not forgiven him for that, making him give his word not to corrupt any other heirs to the Svardian throne.

His phone alerted him to a message from his mother, letting him know that she was set to arrive as planned in the next two days. Finding her had been the easy part. It hadn't taken Theron long to track her down. But it had been a difficult process. His mother had lost many years to alcohol and other addictions and had refused to meet with Lykos.

It had hurt more than he thought he could stand when he'd felt that sense of rejection from his mother—and if Marit hadn't been with him he wasn't sure he'd have survived it. In the end, Kyros had paid a visit to her and had convinced her to let them help her with rehabilitation. For the next few years, she had allowed Kyros and sometimes Theron to meet with her, tell her about the son she had abandoned, and it became clear the guilt and shame she felt over that had been a large contributing factor to her addictions. Patience, time, therapy had slowly begun to ease her feelings and eventually she and Lykos had been able to begin a painfully slow process of getting to know each other again.

But Lykos would never forget what Theron and Kyros had done for him. They had given him the chance to have a relationship with his mother. One late night after the others had gone to bed, on a visit to the Soames estate in Norfolk, England, he and Summer had stayed up, determined to finish the bottle of Limniona, Theron's favourite wine, and he had confessed how much he felt he owed them.

'Love isn't a debt to repay, Lykos.' She'd said it with a hand on his arm and stone-cold clarity in her eyes, before she'd hiccupped and he'd sent her to bed with a laugh. He'd never forgotten her words and instead showered everyone close to him with as much love as possible from that day on.

The doorbell rang, bringing screams of hysterical joy from his two daughters at the bottom of the garden, their little bodies streaking past as they ran to open the door to Theron, Summer and Katy. Lykos went to shift Marit, but she held him in place.

'They've got it, husband.'

'They will terrorise our guests before I can even get a word in,' Lykos warned, well knowing how enthusiastic their daughters could be.

'I know. But there's something I wanted to tell you first.'

'What is it, *agápe mou*? Have you found another instrument you want to learn? Another wedding dress you want to wear? Another list you'd like me to fulfil?'

'Not quite,' she said, biting her lip in that way that always drove him wild. He wasn't concerned in the slightest, because he knew his wife and her rapid heartbeat meant she was excited. Though what she had to be excited about, he... His mind shorted.

'No. Really?' he demanded, launching upward, forcing Marit to cling to his shoulders just to stay upright. 'Are you sure?' he asked, his heart wanting to explode from pure joy. She nodded, sending her crumpled blonde curls into disarray, and he stood up, bringing her with him, and swept her round in a circle.

'We're pregnant again,' Marit whispered and Lykos's heart soared.

Theron, Summer, Katy and their children came to stand at the door to the garden.

'Another one?' Theron demanded.

'Yes,' replied Lykos smugly.

'Seriously?'

Theron spent the rest of the afternoon muttering the word *Rabbits*, and one of the most perfect days Lykos could remember settled into a warm, summery haze of friendship and love as he recalled how it had all started with the Princess who stole the pickpocket's wallet.

* * * * *

WE HOPE YOU ENJOYED
THIS BOOK FROM

⊕ HARLEQUIN
PRESENTS

Escape to exotic locations where passion knows no bounds.

Welcome to the glamorous lives of royals and billionaires, where passion knows no bounds. Be swept into a world of luxury, wealth and exotic locations.

8 NEW BOOKS AVAILABLE EVERY MONTH!

#4021 CINDERELLA IN THE BILLIONAIRE'S CASTLE
Passionately Ever After...
by Clare Connelly

Tormented by the guilt of his past, superrich recluse Thirio has deprived himself of the wild pleasures he once craved. Until Lucinda makes it past the imposing, steel-reinforced doors of his Alpine castle. And now he craves one forbidden night...with her!

#4022 THE PRINCESS HE MUST MARRY
Passionately Ever After...
by Jadesola James

Spare heir Prince Akil's plan is simple: conveniently wed Princess Tobi, gain his inheritance and escape the prison of his royal life. Then they'll go their separate ways. It's going well. Until he finds himself indisputably attracted to his innocent new bride!

#4023 UNDONE BY HER ULTRA-RICH BOSS
Passionately Ever After...
by Lucy King

Exhausted after readying Duarte's Portuguese vineyard for an event, high-end concierge Orla falls asleep between his luxurious sheets. He's clearly unimpressed—but also so ridiculously sexy that she knows the heat between them will be uncontainable...

#4024 HER SECRET ROYAL DILEMMA
Passionately Ever After...
by Chantelle Shaw

After Arielle saved Prince Eirik from drowning, their attraction was instant! Now Arielle faces the ultimate dilemma: indulge in their rare, irresistible connection, knowing her shocking past could taint his royal future...or walk away?

YOU CAN FIND MORE INFORMATION ON UPCOMING HARLEQUIN TITLES, FREE EXCERPTS AND MORE AT HARLEQUIN.COM.

HPCNMRB0522

SPECIAL EXCERPT FROM

(H) HARLEQUIN
PRESENTS

*Tormented by the guilt of his past, superrich recluse
Thirio has deprived himself of the wild pleasures he
once craved. Until Lucinda makes it past the imposing,
steel-reinforced doors of his Alpine castle. And now he
craves one forbidden night…with her!*

*Read on for a sneak preview of
Clare Connelly's next story for Harlequin Presents
Cinderella in the Billionaire's Castle.*

"You cannot leave."

"Why not?"

"The storm will be here within minutes." As if nature
wanted to underscore his point, another bolt of lightning
split the sky in two; a crack of thunder followed. "You
won't make it down the mountain."

Lucinda's eyes slashed to the gates that led to the
castle, and beyond them, the narrow road that had brought
her here. Even in the sunshine of the morning, the drive
had been somewhat hair-raising. She didn't relish the
prospect of skiing her way back down to civilization.

She turned to look at him, but that was a mistake,
because his chest was at eye height, and she wanted to
stare and lose herself in the details she saw there, the
story behind his scar, the sculpted nature of his muscles.
Compelling was an understatement.

"So what do you suggest?" she asked carefully.

"There's only one option." The words were laced with displeasure. "You'll have to spend the night here."

"Spend the night," she repeated breathily. "Here. With you?"

"Not with me, no. But in my home, yes."

"I'm sure I'll be fine to drive."

"Will you?" Apparently, Thirio saw through her claim. "Then go ahead." He took a step backward, yet his eyes remained on her face, and for some reason, it almost felt to Lucinda as though he were touching her.

Rain began to fall, icy and hard. Lucinda shivered.

"I— You're right," she conceded after a beat. "Are you sure it's no trouble?"

"I didn't say that."

"Maybe the storm will clear quickly."

"Perhaps by morning."

"Perhaps?"

"Who knows."

The prospect of being marooned in this incredible castle with this man for any longer than one night loomed before her. Anticipation hummed in her veins.

Don't miss
Cinderella in the Billionaire's Castle,
available July 2022 wherever
Harlequin Presents books and ebooks are sold.

Harlequin.com